Dedalus Eur
General Edito

*Stephanie*

*Herbert Rosendorfer*

# *Stephanie*
## or
# *A Previous Existence*

translated by Mike Mitchell

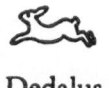

Dedalus

*Dedalus would like to thank Inter Nationes in Bonn for its assistance in producing this translation.*

Published in the UK by Dedalus Ltd, Langford Lodge, St Judith's Lane, Sawtry, Cambs, PE17 5XE

UK ISBN 1 873982 17 8

Distributed in Australia & New Zealand by Peribo Pty Ltd, 58 Beaumont Road, Mount Kuring-gai N.S.W. 2080

Distributed in Canada by Marginal Distribution, Unit 102, 277, George Street North, Peterborough, Ontario, KJ9 3G9

First published in Germany in 1987
First published by Dedalus in 1995

Stephanie © 1987 Nymphenburger Verlagshandlung in F.A. Herbig Verlagsbuchhandlung Gmbh, Munich
Translation copyright © Dedalus 1995

The right of Herbert Rosendorfer to be identified as the author of this work has been asserted by him in accordance with the Copyright, Designs and Patents Act, 1988.

Printed in Finland by Wsoy
Typeset by Datix International Limited, Bungay, Suffolk

This book is sold subject to the condition that it shall not, by way of trade or otherwise, be lent, resold, hired out, or otherwise circulated without the publisher's prior consent in any form of binding or cover other than that in which it is published and without a similar condition including this condition being imposed on the subsequent purchaser.

A C.I.P. listing for this book is available on request.

# Dedalus Europe 1992–95

Dedalus to celebrate the cultural opportunities offered by the single market of the European Union extended its programme of European Literature to include contemporary fiction. This Dedalus Europe 1992–1995 Series has succeeded in making some of the most exciting and original European fiction available for the first time in English.

*Titles currently available include:*

**Night of Amber** – Germain £8.99
**The Book of Nights** – Germain £8.99
**Days of Anger** – Germain £8.99
**The Medusa Child** – Germain £8.99
**The Weeping Woman on the Streets of Prague** – Germain £6.99
**The Black Cauldron** – Heinesen £8.99
**The Architect of Ruins** – Rosendorfer £8.99
**Stephanie** – Rosendorfer £7.99
**A Report of a Murder** – Yatromanolakis £8.99
**The History of a Vendetta** – Yatromanolakis £6.99

*Forthcoming titles include:*

**The Experience of the Night** – Bealu £8.99
**L'Immensités** – Germain £8.99
**Letters Back to Ancient China** – Rosendorfer £8.99

All Dedalus books can be obtained from your local bookshop or newsagent or directly from Dedalus by writing to:
**Cash sales, Dedalus Ltd, Langford Lodge, St Judith's Lane, Sawtry, Cambs, PE17 5XE**
Please enclose a cheque to the value of the books offered + £1 pp for the first book, 75p for each title thereafter up to a maximum of £4.75.

# THE AUTHOR

Herbert Rosendorfer was born in 1934. His first novel *Der Ruinenbaumeister* (1969) was a critical and commercial success and is regarded by many critics as one of the masterpieces of German twentieth century fiction. It was published in English by Dedalus in 1992 as *The Architect of Ruins*.

Herbert Rosendorfer has combined a career as a District Court judge in Munich with the writing of fiction, travel books, and radio and tv plays. His novels *The German Suite* (1972) and *The Night of the Amazons* (1989) have also been translated into English.

Dedalus will publish his novel *Letters back to Ancient China* in 1997.


# THE TRANSLATOR

Mike Mitchell is one of Dedalus's editorial directors and is responsible for Dedalus's translation programme.

His publications include, *The Dedalus Book of Austrian Fantasy: the Meyrink Years 1890–1930; Harrap's German Grammar* and a study of Peter Hacks.

Mike Mitchell's translations include *The Architect of Ruins* by Herbert Rosendorfer, *The Works of Solitude* by Gyorgy Sebystyen and the novels of Gustav Meyrink.

His current projects include translating *Letters back to Ancient China* by Herbert Rosendorfer.

# I

An hour ago I came back from my brother-in-law's funeral. I have to admit that I never liked him. I have several brothers-in-law, since all my sisters are married, but the one I am talking about is Ferdi, the husband of my youngest sister, Stephanie. I took against Ferdi, also sometimes called Ferdl, his real name was Ferdinand, from the first time Stephanie brought him home. I can confess now that at the time I tried to use our parents, surreptitiously and, of course, without success, to wreck the relationship between Stephanie and Ferdi. He wasn't the man for Stephanie, I said. I never did manage to find out what mother's opinion was, for her the only things that counted were facts and not opinions, not even her own. Father's opinion, in this as in all other matters, was one which made things easy for himself, if often irritating for those around him; he believed there was some good in everyone.

The events I am about to relate happened a long time ago. Stephanie had already been married to Ferdi for about ten years when she first told me about her dreams. She never told her husband about them, and with good reason. With his, shall we say, modest intellectual powers he would have thought she was mad. Ferdi never had even the slightest hint of them, although I can say from the outset that there was nothing in them that a wife would need to conceal from her husband. Until now it has never occurred to me to write all this down, even after Stephanie's death. It was only an hour ago, standing by Ferdi's grave, that the idea came to me. It was as if a gate had swung open, clearing the way ahead. I realise now that I didn't want Ferdi ever to hear about these things.

Having said all that, it has become obvious to me that in a way I am doing Ferdi an injustice. He was a simple man; he was also what one calls a 'decent chap'. After Stephanie's death he lived a quiet life, all by himself in that house outside town he was so proud of. He never remarried. They had no children. I didn't see him often, the last time was at the wedding of one of my nieces, the daughter of my eldest sister, but that was four years ago now. He had turned into an old man. That was the first time I thought I might be doing him an injustice. Genuine suffering can give greater depth to even the most rudimentary of characters. Ferdi was a good ten years older than my sister. When I saw him at my niece's wedding he was already well over fifty, but he looked like an old man of seventy. I almost felt sorry for him, and I made a resolution to go and visit him, but it turned out the way things usually do: the years went by and I had other matters to attend to. I never did get round to driving out to G-d-a-. To be precise, I did once drive out there, but I drove past, on the way to somewhere else, and I thought, 'The next time.' I saw the house from a distance. It looked the same as it always had, only more densely ringed with trees and bushes, lots of roses too. Perhaps the roses were Ferdi's hobby after my sister's death.

And now he's dead. I wonder who he's left the house to? I think there were nephews and nieces on his side of the family too, they were people I was never interested in.

I am the only person who was told about my sister's dreams. The remarkable thing about it was not that it was my youngest sister Stephanie, sober, hard-working Stephanie (my mother said of her, 'She's honest, but as dry as stale bread') who had such dreams. The remarkable thing was the way she told me about them. I had gone to see her in their house outside town. Her husband was not at home. She was sitting there in her prefabricated house in which everything that could be was made of plastic and where washability was the most important criterion. She was sitting in a chair, knitting or crocheting. We were talking about things that had nothing to do with dreams or such matters, when all at once she stopped knitting or whatever and said, 'Do you know, I've been having these funny dreams.'

She said it as if she were talking about a phenomenon which she had been thinking about for some time, but which was rather out of the way and did not really concern her; as if she had said, 'Tell me, do we have a new vicar, or has the old one just started wearing a wig?'

'*How* funny?' I asked.

She had taken up her knitting again, but let it sink back into her lap. 'A month ago. Not roughly a month ago, exactly a month ago today. I dreamt I was waking up. That does happen, you know, dreaming that you're waking up. I woke up. It was night, quite dark. I was lying in bed, of course. We have duvets . . .' (machine washable, I thought) '. . . in my dream I ran my hand over the duvet, but it wasn't the duvet. It was an eiderdown with a damask cover. Can you remember that dark wardrobe with the griffons on?'

She was talking about our grandparents' house. Of course I could remember those ugly griffons.

'Grandmother kept her trousseau in it. She showed it me once. There was damask bed-linen, all hand-sewn with embroidered monograms the size of side-plates. There were some that she had never used. 'I was keeping those', she said. 'What for . . .?' 'For your mother', she said. But when mother got married that kind of heavy damask bed-linen wasn't the kind of thing a young couple would want any more. I wonder what became of it?'

'And what happened next in your dream?'

'Nothing at all. I just gently stroked the damask bed-linen. It was very fine damask, not the heavy sort like grandmother's, you can tell, even in the dark. I knew I wasn't in my own bed. Then I must have gone back to sleep; that is, I must have dreamt that I went back to sleep.'

Stephanie picked up her knitting. For a while she said nothing, then, 'And the unpleasant thing about it was that in my dream, and also afterwards, when I woke up in the morning, I had the feeling that I hadn't been dreaming at all. I felt I really was awake, I really was somewhere else.'

(She didn't say 'the uncanny thing about it', or 'the eerie thing', she said, 'the unpleasant thing'.)

I found it difficult to ask her about it because it is the kind of thing to which one would prefer not to receive an answer. I am different from my sister.

I asked, 'And . . . did you have the dream again?'

'Yes', she said, 'the very next night. Again I dreamt I was waking up. Again I could feel the fine damask cover, but this time it wasn't completely dark. The long, heavy curtain over a window was drawn back just a tiny bit. It must have been day already, I mean early morning, very early in the morning. It wasn't moonlight, it was daylight, pale, early morning light, the first light of dawn, a greyish light. It was perfectly quiet, the only sound was the rustle of the damask cover when I ran my hand over it. The strip of grey light ran right across the room, it was a very large room, much larger than our bedroom. The strip of light went from the curtain right across the room, diagonally across the room, and at the side of the bed there was a dull, golden gleam from some object like the frame of a large picture.'

'You didn't see anything else?'

'I . . . I was afraid. This time again I had the feeling I wasn't dreaming, I swear to you I felt I was awake, really awake. I didn't dare move, and nothing else moved, either. I wouldn't have dared move a muscle. Then I went back to sleep.'

'Are you sure that was the day after? You're sure it wasn't the same dream?'

'Quite sure. I dreamt it on the next day as well, for the third time. I was afraid even before I went to sleep, but I couldn't say anything about it to Ferdi, he'd think I was mad. Have I gone mad?'

'What was the third dream like?'

'Just like the other two, except the curtain was open a little wider. There was a broader strip of grey, dawn light falling across the room. Again that gleam of gold. I did turn my eyes a little, that much I did manage. It was a painting with a heavy, carved, gilt frame; the picture itself I couldn't see. Below the picture there was a dark chest of drawers with brass fittings which also gleamed. After I had been lying there awake for a while, a bird started singing outside. I've never heard a bird sing like that. I couldn't see the bird. Nothing moved, and I didn't move either, except I very gently stroked the damask cover and turned my eyes, just my eyes, not my head. You wouldn't have moved, either, in that situation. For a few days after nothing happened. I thought the nonsense had stopped, but a week after the third dream, it was back. The curtain was half drawn back from the window. There was a fine muslin curtain rippling in the wind. For the first time I saw the bed. I've never slept in a bed like that in my whole life, it was very wide, an enormous bed. I was on the left-hand side, but I didn't dare look to the right, not for all the saints in heaven.'

'Did the bird start singing again?'

'The bird didn't sing again, but when the wind got up a little, just a gentle breeze that set the muslin curtain fluttering, suddenly there was the scent of oranges. I took my courage in both hands – 'Even if I die of fright', is what I thought to myself – and looked upwards and behind me. I still didn't dare look to the right, not yet, but up and behind. And there I saw a huge carved crucifix. It was hanging over the bed. The following nights there wasn't much new. Occasionally the bird sang; if the wind blew, the muslin curtains rippled and there was a scent of oranges. Yesterday I'd had enough. I didn't know what to do. A body needs her sleep. I wondered whether to sleep in a chair here in the living room but, my God I thought, where might I wake up then? If it had to happen, I'd rather be in bed. But I did make up my mind that if I dreamt again I would sit up. I did sit up. And I looked to the right. There was a man beside me in that huge bed. It wasn't Ferdi. It was a man who was dead.'

# II

Our father was a minor civil servant. His life was a scornful commentary on the common opinion of civil servants: he died of heart failure before he reached sixty. The damask bed-covers came from the family of our maternal grandparents, our paternal grandparents had, at best, linen ones. Because he was a civil servant, during the Nazi period our father had to obtain a so-called 'Certificate of Aryan Descent'. He collected the documents he needed, and later on they were still lying around at home. I saw them once. Father's ancestors were craftsmen and farm labourers, such insignificant people that their trail petered out in the illegible murk of parish registers and public records offices around the turn of the eighteenth and nineteenth centuries. Our maternal ancestors were definitely superior, there were farmers among them, 'householders' and 'landowners'. Our father had married slightly above his station, not that that was a problem in the marriage, as far as I could remember. We all got so-called 'good' jobs. Stephanie was a qualified physiotherapist. She was very competent and everywhere she worked she was well-liked and received glowing references. She had also been a star pupil, at primary school, secondary school, everywhere. When I was in my last years at secondary school and she was just starting primary and coming home with nothing but straight 'A's as if there were no other grades, whilst I had fair-to-middling marks, not alarming, but not particularly exciting either, I used to think – later on I said it out loud – 'Thank God she's *younger*'. If an *older* sister had had such outstanding results she would have been held up as a very depressing 'shining example'. But Stephanie wasn't a swot, nor was she a goody-goody, and she had her share of experiences. Since she was pretty – perhaps even beautiful, a brother is not the best judge – there was no shortage of boyfriends. With some it almost ripened into an engagement.

And she was involved in all kinds of smart activities, she played tennis, took riding lessons, one whole summer she even played golf with a boyfriend of the sports-car type, and for a time she was a real night-bird. But she never cut herself off completely from the family, never fled the nest like her sisters, who all left home before they got married, set up in a flat of their own and led an independent life. Stephanie stayed at home until she met Ferdi in the hospital she worked in, where he was recovering from the effects of a car accident.

I don't deny that from the very beginning I had the feeling that my sister too had . . . no, no, that's not the kind of thing one says nowadays, 'married beneath her station'. But she had, I thought, and still do think, sold herself for less than her true value.

There was nothing wrong with Ferdi, he wasn't a womaniser or anything like that, quite the contrary. But he was intellectually limited. He was stupid. I don't deny, either – at least not now, I would have then, and at the top of my voice – that another reason I didn't like my new brother-in-law was because he had quite a lot of money, by our standards. Not that I object to other people having money, but I feel it is wrong when people like Ferdi, with their limited intellectual resources, earn the kind of money which other, more intelligent people don't have – and to avoid misunderstanding, I must emphasise that I am not referring to myself. Ferdi was a lorry-driver and there was one point in his life when fortune had smiled on him; and you have to grant that he recognised the stroke of luck in a situation which others would have seen as a misfortune. Once he had been away on a long journey with his lorry. When he set off, the transport firm he worked for was apparently sound; when he came back, two weeks later, it had been closed down. The haulage contractor had been declared bankrupt, something of rarity in those days of the 'economic miracle'. Ferdi did not leave his lorry parked outside the sealed gates of the firm, but drove home in it. He went through the proper channels and declared it to the receiver, who offered it to him as compensation for the wages he was due. Ferdi jumped at the opportunity, and that's how he became his own boss. When he married my sister he already had several lorries and employed a number of drivers. Hard-working he certainly was, but he was one of those people who, when they get home, are only interested in the armchair and the odd television programme, as long it's not something they'll find disturbing; one of those people who don't know what to do if it rains on a Saturday; one of those people who, if it's not raining on a Sunday, will set off in anorak and rucksack along an easy path through the hills frightening the cows, have a piece of cake in a tea-shop and then, in the evening, after they've seen nothing and done nothing, say, 'Wasn't that a lovely day.'

Perhaps everything would have been different if Stephanie and Ferdi had had children. Of course I've no idea why they didn't, whether they didn't want any, or whether there was something wrong with him or with my sister. One thing you have to say, Ferdi would certainly have made a good father. People like him, whose intellectual horizons are close enough for them to touch with their outstretched hands, are often fond of children. Earlier on, before Stephanie's strange death, I occasionally observed him playing with our nephews and nieces. It almost made me feel I should make him a silent apology. Would Stephanie have been a good mother? Perhaps, given how sober and capable she was, perhaps not, for the very same reasons. Anyway, there weren't any children, so there Stephanie was, in her off-the-peg, prefabricated house, all fitted out in plastic, with what you might call a stain-resistant, drip-dry garden, and with nothing to do. She never complained she was bored, on the contrary, I once asked her and she said no, she wasn't bored at all. She did this and she did that . . . It is possible it was this repressed boredom which came out in her mysterious dreams. That would have been one explanation, if it hadn't been for all the other, tangible things which were certainly not dreams.

'I was so shocked, I couldn't move a muscle, of course', Stephanie said, 'but also I was more certain than ever that I was not dreaming, that I was awake.'

'How did you know the man was dead?'

'That I'd rather not say.'

'Did you just assume the man was dead, or did you think you were sure?'

'No, no. He was dead. I could see. I don't want to think about it any more. I've worked in hospitals for long enough, the man wasn't the first dead body I've seen. Very gently I let myself back down on to the pillows. I wanted to think about what to do next . . . and that's how I must have gone back to sleep again.'

'You've told Ferdi about this?'

'No.'

'Of course, you were dreaming all the time.'

'Of course.'

'You were dreaming that you had a distinct feeling you were not dreaming.'

'Yes.'

'Are you afraid . . .'

'I'm terrified.'

'You must tell Ferdi about it.'

'What could Ferdi do?'

'Tell him to wake you up.'

'When? Every half hour? Every ten minutes?'

'You're quite right, it was a silly idea. And sleeping in another room . . . you said yourself there was the danger . . .'

'It's something else I'm afraid of.'

'What else?'

'That there'll . . . that there'll come a time when I have to stay *there*. *There* is not quite the right word for it. When I'm dreaming I'm not just somewhere else, I'm some*when* else, I'm in a different time. And I very much fear I'm some*one* else as well.'

'That's not very easy to follow', I said.

'In dreams everything's possible', said Stephanie with a laugh. By day she could even laugh at her dreams. (To be precise, in the mornings and up to four o'clock, she told me; after four o'clock things changed and she couldn't laugh at them any more.) 'In dreams everything's possible.'

'What were you wearing?'

'In bed? A nightie like I always do.'

'*There* as well?'

'I didn't pay any attention to that, but when I think back, I have the feeling I was wearing a nightdress there as well.'

'The same nightdress?'

'That I couldn't say.'

'I assume you keep your wedding ring on at night?'

'Yes – but I couldn't say whether I was still wearing it there.'

'You should keep an eye open for that kind of thing.'

'But I don't want it to happen again.'

I tried to reassure my sister. As long as it was light, she was not afraid, but as soon as evening came, the fears returned. Sleep is unavoidable. It was no use not going to bed. There was *one* thing that would have helped, but neither of us knew that at the time. In spite of everything, I tried to reassure Stephanie with empty phrases such as, 'Don't take it to heart', 'Perhaps you've seen the last of it', 'Life is but an empty dream', 'We'll have a good laugh at it next time I come'. There was something else that had occurred to me; I have to admit that somewhere at the back of my mind was the idea (an idea I was soon to feel ashamed of ever having entertained), that she was going round the bend. No, 'going round the bend', that's what Ferdi would have said. What I had in mind was some kind of obscure mental illness, hallucinations caused by the boredom she refused to admit to. I have heard that such hallucinations have to be taken seriously, or at least you should behave as if you do take them seriously. Perhaps it will help her, I remember thinking, if I encourage her in these fantasies. I had just reached this conclusion when Stephanie said,

'You think I'm mad too?'

'No, no', I said quickly. Then I tried to convince her that attack was the best form of defence, so to speak. 'I'm not coming to any conclusion, for the moment. It could be this, could be that.' I tried to persuade her to observe everything in her bedroom *there*, to take note of details (nightdress, wedding-ring etc) and, if she could bring herself to it, to get out of bed and look out of the window. She made no promises, but I said I would come back the next day.

When I said goodbye, Stephanie held out her hand to me, but did not look up from her knitting. I knew my way out.

The idea of having a quiet word with Ferdi about it I rejected the moment it occurred to me.

# III

G-d-a- is not beautiful, nor is it ugly. In the fifteen years that have passed since these events, they have built large new estates, including high-rise buildings, in G-d-a-, all for people who work in the city. It's on the urban railway network now. People who live in G-d-a- now practically live in the city. At the time when Ferdi bought the house in G-d-a- it was 'a long way out', much too far for people who had to travel in to work every day. G-d-a- is situated where the land is still flat, but not completely flat, you can see the wooded hills. It is not one of the neat, pert highland villages, it is a haphazard collection of incomers' houses with their pointed gables and well-groomed gardens. There are often dogs yapping beside the green wire-netting fences. In the gardens the flowers bloom, and on weekdays the revolving clothes lines sprout underpants. On Sundays the women sit on the patios in flowered overalls, the men in track-suits or shorts (although, with their fat thighs and bald heads, they are long past the age of shorts), drinking coffee and eating cakes. They are the kind of houses where you would say, if you were visiting them for the first time, 'Isn't it nice here?'

When I drove out to see Stephanie the next day, that is the day after she first told me about her strange dreams (my work allows me a great deal of freedom in organising my time, even on weekdays), it was not yet the season for sitting out on the patio. It was the end of March and the weather was, if anything, cold. There had even been some snow a few days earlier, and the women in their flowered housecoats and the men who, later in the year, would sit out on the patios in shorts or track-suits, were more concerned about their plants and were anxiously wrapping their more sensitive bushes in swathes of perforated plastic.

Stephanie was not wearing a flowered housecoat, she didn't go that far (Ferdi, on the other hand, often went around at home in a dark burgundy track-suit with white stripes along the sides, the seat of which sagged down to his knees). Ferdi wasn't there. Stephanie was busying herself cleaning the already sparkling windows and therefore saw me from a long way off and had cleared away the buckets and wash-leathers before I reached the door. She was in a sparkling mood herself.

The more I thought about her revelations the previous day, the more disturbing I found them. Not that they had given me a sleepless night, my sleep is always stronger than any worries, but I had spent almost all my waking hours between the two visits thinking about them. I decided that the first thing I would do when I arrived would be to ask her if she had had another dream. Assuming, of course, that Ferdi was not there.

Now, seeing Stephanie so bright and cheerful, I wished the whole affair simply hadn't happened. This feeling was so strong that I just could not put the question, so I began by talking of unimportant matters. However, Stephanie brought it up herself in a tone of puzzled amusement, as if she were saying, 'Just imagine, today I washed the first volume of the Goethe in the machine by mistake!' – which, in fact, had once happened to her because Ferdi had somehow managed to get the book mixed up with his dirty shirts, something unheard of in such a well-regulated household. They had never managed to work out exactly how it had happened. After it had been through the wash, the Goethe presented a remarkable sight: the binding was all warped and the pages stuck out in all directions, forming an almost perfect circle. I suggested they keep the spherical volume as a rarity, but Stephanie threw it away.

Stephanie said, 'Just imagine, I got out of bed.'

And she told me what had happened.

As in all her previous dreams she was lying in bed, in the fine damask bed-linen. She immediately remembered my suggestion and looked at her hands. (Though she did make sure not to look to the right.) She was wearing her wedding-ring, and the other ring on her left hand that Ferdi had given her as a wedding-anniversary present. She was also wearing a nightdress, but not the one she had put on earlier that evening. It had been very cold yesterday, she explained, and Ferdi had to sleep with the window open or he would snore, so she had been wearing a fairly thick jersey nightie. But when she looked to see what she was wearing *there*, it was a very fine cambric nightdress with voluminous sleeves and lace around the neck and cuffs. In spite of that, she didn't feel cold, even though the window was open there too. It was very quiet. The strange bird hadn't been singing, but the scent of oranges that came from the widow was very strong.

Very carefully she turned back the light eiderdown and got out of bed. The floor was cool, a stone floor in a regular pattern of red and white. By the bed was a pair of black embroidered mules with no backs and high heels. She felt rather uncomfortable wearing the slippers, but, she thought, it would have been even more uncomfortable to walk barefoot across the tiled floor, even if it wasn't cold out of bed. Beside the bed was a small black cupboard, elaborately turned and carved, presumably a bedside cabinet. On the bedside table was a book, bound in parchment but without a cover illustration or title on the front.

No, she said in answer to my question, she had not touched the book.

Next to the bedside cabinet was a candlestick almost the height of a man, with a thick candle in it that had more or less completely burnt down. The candlestick was gilt, like a candlestick in a church.

Although she walked very carefully, the mules made a clatter on the stone floor because of the high heels.

'You mustn't forget', said Stephanie, 'that in spite of my curiosity I kept on thinking, 'There's a dead man in the bed'.'

She was going to go over to the window first of all, but then she remembered what I had said about taking note of everything. So first she had a look at the picture in the heavy gold frame. It was a fairly large picture, dark and, to her mind anyway, not particularly beautiful. Pictured on it were various female saints, probably the infant Jesus as well.

What, from the bed, she had taken for a window, was a door, a glass door. It was partly open and the curtain — not black, as she had assumed at first, but very dark green — was drawn back. On the other side of the door was a muslin curtain which the breeze was blowing into the opening, making it billow out like a delicate sail.

She pulled back the muslin curtain as well and, without letting go of it, took a small step out onto the terrace.

By that time she wasn't afraid any more.

The view stretched into the distance. Immediately in front of the house — palace would be a more appropriate word — was a garden. The scent of oranges, which was even stronger on the terrace than in the bedroom, came from this garden. There were cypresses towering up among the orange trees. Along the paths to the side of the palace were countless roses in bloom, in all imaginable shades of red, orange and white.

It was not an Italian garden, and definitely not a French one. It was a wild garden, a tamed wilderness. The sea of roses did not look as if it had been planted and tended, rather it was as if a wilderness of roses had been thinned and pruned and laboriously trained in rows, canalised, so to speak. It wasn't an English garden, either, it was not a cool park, but a luxuriant, blazing garden. She already had an idea where it was, she said, she'd tell me that later.

The nearer part of the garden was still in the shadow of the large house or palace. From that she assumed the terrace faced west and the sun rose behind her, behind the house. The palace threw long shadows. It must have been early in the morning. Given that, it was not surprising that there was no one to be seen and nothing to be heard apart from the splash of a fountain. The fountain itself she could not see.

The sky was cloudless. It was the morning of a day that promised to be very hot. A pale sickle moon hung over the western horizon, which was bounded by wild and barren mountains. They were not rocky mountains like the ones we have here, but more rounded ones, of gravel or scree. There were also similar mountains to the south, their higher summits covered in snow.

The countryside beyond the garden, which was obviously immense, was of an earthy brown, almost red colour and fairly bare, although there were patches of woodland dotted about. She couldn't, she said, see any villages, just the occasional small, rather dilapidated, clay-coloured cottage.

Only to the left, in a dip between wooded hills that looked like continuations of the garden, could she see a largish town. There were cathedrals and churches towering up out of a sea of reddish and clay-coloured houses. On a hill which, in contrast to the rest, was thickly wooded and stuck into the city like a wedge, there was a group of red buildings, part palace, part temple. Jerusalem! was the thought that went through her mind. It could only be Jerusalem.

There was a second hill, almost conical and bare of trees, cutting into the city from the other side. On this hill there was a church. All the buildings cast long shadows, only the highest towers and the church on the hill were in the golden light of dawn. It was a beautiful, but also a gloomy scene.

'Somehow', Stephanie said, 'I had a sense of the desert. It wasn't a Christian city, in spite of all the domes and spires. It was an oriental city. It can only have been Jerusalem.'

'I know Jerusalem', I said. 'It doesn't look like that.'

'I can't imagine that it's any other city than Jerusalem.' It is remarkable that Stephanie did not realise straight away which city it really (really?) was, given that it had played an important part in the life of our mother and therefore, indirectly, in ours during our childhood, although none of us actually saw it as a child.

There was a flight of stone steps, she went on, leading from the end of the terrace down into the garden. But she didn't dare go down them, firstly because she was afraid she might for some reason never get back up, and secondly because of what she was wearing, nothing but the extremely fine, thin nightdress.

The terrace and the steps had an elaborate stone balustrade. On the terrace there were two stone benches, and on the balustrade of the terrace a small statue, a bearded apostle. ('They must have been very devout people', she said.)

She must, she thought, have stood there for more than a quarter of an hour, so immersed in the beautiful yet gloomy landscape that she had forgotten who, or, rather, what was in the bed in the room behind her to which she would have to return: a dead man, '. . . more than a dead man.'

'What do you mean?' I asked. 'Several dead men?'

'No', she said, 'one man who was more than dead.'

'There's no such thing as . . .'

'Yes there is', she said. 'More than dead.'

After she had been standing on the terrace for a while, she shivered, not so much because she was wearing nothing but the gossamer nightdress, as because she was suddenly afraid the room behind her might have changed, so that she would not be able to find her way back. But the room was just the same, and the moment she stepped into it, she knew what had happened the evening before.

'I wasn't dreaming. In dreams you can't just go through a door when you want to. I wasn't dreaming.'

'And what had happened the evening before.'

Stephanie shook her head.

After a while she went on with her story.

When she went back into the bedroom, she felt tired. She had taken that as a sign to prepare herself for her return *here*. In spite of that, she went over to one of the large, black double doors, to the door on the same side of the room as her side of the bed. She opened the door. It led into a vestibule that was more or less empty. After some hesitation she cautiously opened the next door, but she just put her head round it. Inside was a huge drawing-room with beautiful old furniture. One piece that struck her particularly was a black cabinet with strange decorations standing against the wall on the left. It had reminded her of something – of what she would tell me in a minute. The floor was very beautiful as well. It was also of stone, but whereas the one in the bedroom only had red and white squares, this one was richly and elaborately decorated, a mosaic floor, almost like a Persian carpet, with brightly coloured flowers stretching from wall to wall, a petrified flower garden.

Then, she said, she closed the doors carefully and went back to bed. Whether she would have been capable of getting back into the bed and stretching out beside the gruesome corpse – even more gruesome since she knew what had happened the evening before – if she had not been overcome with weariness, that she could not say. As it was, in her weary state, it had almost seemed like coming home. She had fallen asleep straight away.

'And what did the cabinet remind you of?'

'Of Aunt Helen . . .'

# IV

Aunt Helen was actually Great -aunt Helen, a sister of our grandmother on our mother's side, from the damask line. None of us had known her (we were all born after she died), but there was no one in the family about whom there were more stories; it is a reasonable suspicion that over the years they became increasingly mythical. I will try to limit myself to those that sound credible, even if they occasionally have an air of fantasy.

Our branch of grandmother's very extended family (she was the seventeenth child of her parents) had a closer connection than others to Aunt Helen in that she was mother's godmother. One of the family mementoes we found among grandmother's possessions after her death was an old photograph showing Aunt Helen surrounded by a number of children (which I will talk about in a moment). The similarity to Stephanie is unmistakable.

Our grandmother came from Austria, where her ancestors had been landowners. Mother occasionally used to talk of a silver mine that her great-great-grandfather was supposed to have had, more than that she did not know. Great-grandfather is supposed to have been a member of the Austrian Imperial Diet for a while. He used to boast, she said, that everything he and his family, also counting the servants, ate and wore (with the exception of coffee) had been grown on their own land. I might as well add here that not a penny of all this wealth came to us. The financial decline seems to have begun with great-grandfather. Grandmother used to mutter about disastrous speculations, ill-considered sureties and a fateful penchant for driving four-in-hand. Hardly had he bought a new team – all four horses had to be exactly the same – than one would promptly go lame, contract glanders, the staggers or the heaves and expire. The remaining three would be worth less than three-quarters of the price of the complete team, but in his annoyance great-grandfather would sell them off dirt cheap and buy a new team, and the whole process would repeat itself. Great-grandfather must also have had problems with his sons, there were incredible stories in circulation. But that was all a long time ago, even grandmother only knew them from hearsay. There were some brothers and sisters she had never met; she was thirty years younger than her eldest brother.

That Aunt Helen took a 'position' – as did our grandmother after her – is presumably connected with the fact that the effects of the financial decline were already making themselves felt on the family's way of life. From her childhood on, our aunt seems to have had a tendency towards eccentricity. Once a circus visited the town and the younger children and grandchildren were allowed to go and see it. The next day the circus moved on and Aunt Helen, about nine years old at the time, disappeared. Given the large number of children in the family, her disappearance was not noticed at first, but when it was, the correct inference was immediately drawn. Great-grandfather harnessed the current four-in-hand and tore down the valley until he caught up with the circus. Aunt Helen was practising on the tightrope.

She was sent to a boarding school run by Catholic nuns. A bare six months later she had become so pious that she had decided to follow the career (if that is the right word) of a nun. That did not at all suit great-grandfather, who was more of an upper-class liberal. He took his eccentric daughter away from the Catholic nuns and sent her to one of the few, but highly regarded Protestant girls' schools in Austria. The inevitable followed: six months later Helen wanted to convert to Protestantism. Great-grandfather's liberalism seems to have had its limits; Helen was brought back home.

The 'position' which Aunt Helen later took was, of course, one befitting the family's station in society. First she was 'companion' to a Countess P. in Vienna, where her main duty consisted of reading aloud, then she went to the wife of a Jewish baron who, among other things, had a villa in Bad Ischl. That, of course, was where the Emperor Franz-Josef spent the summer, and in those days everybody who was anybody had a villa in Ischl. That appears to have been the setting – though all one heard were rumours, even to my mother Aunt Helen only gave vague hints – for a decisive experience, which was a turning point in the life of our aunt, who must have been around 20 at the time. The focus of this experience is presumed to have been a young, exceptionally good-looking officer, who was beyond the lawful reach of all women: he was a Teutonic Knight, consequently in holy orders. Aunt Helen gave up her position with Baroness M. Given her social background and upbringing, any other than a lawful union would have been out of the question for her.

The whole, presumably sad story only became known in the family because grandmother had reached the age where she, too, was about to 'take a position'. She was her sister's successor in Baroness M.'s household, and there she also became acquainted with the officer in holy orders. 'A fine figure of a man', she used to say, 'when he went to church on Sundays in his long white robe with the black cross on the side of his chest and his sabre at his side . . .' He was, she added, very grave and well-educated. 'There is nothing', she said, 'that causes a woman's heart such sweet sorrow as love for a man no woman can have.' I assume she was referring to Aunt Helen. During the whole of the rest of her life there was no hint of any further 'experiences'.

She went to France to be governess to the family of the Duc de B., in particular to look after their youngest child, who was an epileptic. It is probably a sign of a change in outlook that, after the more vacuous employment with bored Countesses and Baronesses, she took on this serious task. The photograph that I mentioned before comes from this time. In it there are half a dozen princes and princesses standing in the garden, the boys in sailor suits, the girls in white dresses. Aunt Helen is in white, too, she is the only one sitting, beautiful and grave; her eyes are shaded by the straight brim of a somewhat stern straw hat, in her left hand she is holding a rolled-up parasol, in her right the hand of the smallest of the boys, presumably the epileptic child.

The next story concerning Aunt Helen is not the subject of vague rumours; on the contrary, it is told with pride. It is the pride of the whole family. Not every family has something like this in its history.

A regular visitor to the house of the Duke was the Comte de Paris, the head of the House of Bourbon, the same who would have been *Roi de France et de Navarre* if history had stuck to the legitimist track. This Comte de Paris pursued the beautiful Austrian governess with what they called at that time his unwelcome attentions. Again Aunt Helen left her position and moved to Italy, where she took a position as governess with the family of Count Ch. The Ch.'s lived in Siena in the summer, in the winter in Rome. It was during the winter that Aunt Helen changed employers, which meant she went to Rome. On one of her first free days she did what every visitor to Rome does as a matter of course, she went to St. Peter's. (This description of the climax of our family history follows that of my grandmother, who had the details at first hand from her sister.) It was a weekday, and a dull, somewhat rainy November day at that, so there was hardly anyone else in the church. Aunt Helen had already been in the church for some time, looking at this and that; all there had been were a few subordinate priests scurrying to and fro with rat-like gait, sketching a routine genuflection before the statue of a saint as they did so, or twitching an altar-cloth straight; then, when she was already making her way towards the exit, she noticed in the damp November twilight beside the Stuart mausoleum a man who was very clearly not one of the scurrying acolytes. He was walking with a stick and examining the memorials on the left and on the right.

'He limps', grandmother told us Aunt Helen thought to herself, 'just like the Comte de Paris.'

It was the Comte de Paris.

He was not at all surprised to see Aunt Helen, since it was because of her that he had made the journey from Paris to Rome. He knelt down and offered our aunt his hand in marriage. An offer of marriage from the Comte de Paris in

St. Peter's in Rome! What family has that to show for itself? And our aunt refused him.

'Why?' grandmother had asked.

'Because not only did he have a gammy leg', said Aunt Helen, 'he also used to dribble his food.'

It could be that was only the ostensible reason.

The war – or, to be more precise, Italy's entry into the war – put an end to Aunt Helen's employment with the Ch. family. Aunt Helen was an Austrian citizen and, if she did not want to be interned, had to leave Italy. She obviously did not want to go back to Austria, so she booked a passage for Spain, which was neutral. The Ch's had relatives among the Spanish aristocracy and gave her recommendations. Aunt Helen found a position with the family of a Duke of I. and stayed there for many years, even after the Duke's children had long since grown up.

There is one more story from Aunt Helen's childhood. A friend of great-grandfather's who was also his lawyer in the provincial capital regularly used to spend his summer holidays with the family in great-grandfather's house in Z. The lawyer's son, a particularly small and ugly child who, moreover, had red hair and the, for that region, rather exotic name of Wilfried (he was known as 'Willa'), had been taken with a childish affection, a kind of scale model of an adult passion, for Aunt Helen. Willa was twelve, Helen eight. Astonishingly, Helen returned his affection. For one whole summer the two children were inseparable. Doing everything together with such a tidy and well-behaved boy as Willa, grandmother said, had made Helen, the tomboy, as quiet as a lamb. When the holidays were over, the two children had cried their hearts out and sworn to spend the next summer in each other's company. That did not happen, however; for some reason or other, that was the last summer the lawyer spent in Z. with his children.

Wilfried passed his school-leaving examinations with distinction, studied law and passed those exams with similar distinction, and was his parents' pride and joy, even though his looks did not improve with age and he became if anything even more red-haired, until he began to go bald around thirty, by which time he had gained his doctorate *magna cum laude*. He didn't take over his father's practice, but became a judge, had a brilliant career, married, sent his children to university, ended up as President of the Central Provincial Court in Graz, and retired. He never forgot Helen.

It must have been in the years around 1930 that Aunt Helen returned home for the first time in forty years. Her parents had died long ago, the house had been sold, the fields and woods were in other hands, her brothers and sisters scattered all over the continent. There were a few gravestones left to recall the family that had once owned half the village. The old priest, who still remembered Helen, showed her the sumptuous altar-cloths her mother had embroidered and given to the church. They were treasured, he said, and only used on special feast-days.

Aunt Helen, now an old woman, took a room at the inn and stayed for a few days. She went for walks through the village and up the gentle, lush green hills to where the sparse pine-woods began in which her father had gone hunting. She liked to sit on the bench outside a chapel that her grandfather had had built at this spot, from which you could see the whole village lying among the fields with their hedges and fences. Every field shone in a different shade of green. After the village, the road led down into the dark valley that only opened out into the wide, fruitful plain, with its broader acres and larger towns, beyond the world-famous gorge in which the wild water foamed against the splintered red rocks.

Her favourite time for sitting there was the late morning. The bench stood in the shadow of a tall beech, a huge old tree with a bizarre shape which, seen from the east at dusk against the fading light, formed fantastic faces, the heads of old men or gargoyles, but which now, at midday, rose up into the sky like a friendly tower of green. Helen would sit there musing until the midday chimes roused her from her thoughts. Then she would go back down to take her lunch in the inn. (The man who ran the inn was too young to remember her, but had heard of her. The old innkeeper however, who had handed over the inn to his son years ago but still lived there, when he heard that Helen had come, for all his ninety years, got someone to take him to her and greeted her with deep reverence. He was old enough still to have been a tenant of her father's.)

One day during the second week of her stay, when she came down from the bench beside the little chapel, Aunt Helen found Dr. Wilfried S. sitting in the inn. He had somehow heard about her visit and had driven up.

He was, our grandmother had been told by her sister, completely bald and wore a brown check suit consisting of knickerbockers and a kind of Norfolk jacket with a belt. She had been extremely surprised to see him, said Aunt Helen, but had recognised him immediately. They spent more than a week together in Z. and decided to get married the next year. Aunt Helen wanted to spend another year in Spain after which she had intended to retire from her position anyway. Uncle Willa (mother called him that, despite the fact that strictly speaking he was not our uncle, but had merely almost become an uncle by marriage) accompanied her as far as Genoa.

The following winter Aunt Helen decided to teach her grown-up charges, the three children of the Duke of I., the waltz, the real, genuine Viennese waltz, which is presumably not so widely known in Spain. In the course of a lesson she slipped on the stone floor and fell so awkwardly that her foot ended up under a heavy cabinet, leaving her leg with a very complicated lateral fracture. Perhaps the doctor who treated her was incompetent, perhaps she already had some other, latent complaint which was brought on by her long period lying in bed, but whatever the cause, she died in the spring. Grandmother was with her during those last few weeks, having been apprised of her aunt's illness by a very formal letter from the Duke's majordomo. Our mother, at that time a young girl of fourteen, went with her. Grandmother sent a telegram to Dr. S. 'Don't tell him', Aunt Helen had begged, 'it'll only cause him unnecessary worry. When I'm better I'll be going back with you anyway.'

The Duke decreed that in consideration of her long, faithful service Aunt Helen should be buried in the ducal vault in the cathedral – in the side vault for superior domestics. Granada was the city where she had died. The Duke and the Duchess in person, as well as the princes and princesses, paid their last respects to Aunt Helen. Dr. S. was beside himself with grief, which, however, – 'He was a fascinating man, but must have been terribly pedantic' mother said – did not hinder him from spending the next few days, Baedecker in hand, systematically doing the sights of Granada. He checked all the dimensions given in the guide by pacing them out, and he discovered that Baedecker was one out in the number of steps in the bell-tower of the cathedral. When he reached the top of the tower, the first thing Uncle Willa did, even before enjoying the view, was to correct the statement in the book.

Shortly afterwards Uncle Willa moved from Graz to Z. – he had, you will remember, already retired – where he built a small house on the edge of the village. Our mother, for whom Dr. S. had developed a friendly affection – she was, of course, the godchild of his childhood sweetheart and perhaps resembled her –, was several times invited to spend the holidays with him. He had, she told us, made a regular cult of Aunt Helen. He built a stone wall round the little bench by the chapel, so that it was shielded from wind and weather. In the wall behind the bench the words 'Helen's Rest' were carved. Every day in the late morning, and often again in the evenings before sunset, Uncle Willa would go up there.

He also had a coffee cup with a picture of Aunt Helen on it. He had had it specially made in Vienna from a photograph of her. He only drank out of that cup.

I knew exactly what Stephanie meant when she said, 'Of Aunt Helen . . .'

The trip to Granada was mother's first long journey and remained the longest journey she made during her whole life. She liked talking about it and remembered every detail.

She had been presented to the Duke and Duchess. The chamberlain had shown her the place where Aunt Helen had fallen.

'It was a large room', mother told us, 'almost a ballroom. The most beautiful thing about it was the floor. It was a stone floor, a sumptuous mosaic of many small stones, like a petrified flower garden.'

'So what you saw', I said, 'wasn't Jerusalem, but Granada.'

# V

I am single. I travel a lot, and already did so at the time of Stephanie's revelations. My work involved travelling, but I also used every holiday for some trip. I had been to many parts of the world, but not yet, at that time, to southern Spain. If one had marked out my journeys on a map – the thought came to me during my flight from Madrid to Granada in an old-fashioned propeller machine that did not exactly inspire confidence – one might well perhaps have come to the conclusion that I had deliberately avoided this country, had given it a wide berth. And that in spite of the fact that, as it had played such a brief but important part in our mother's life, I had been aware of Granada and its beauty since my earliest childhood. Once, Uncle Willa, who never forgot a birthday among his relatives and friends, gave mother a study of the art of the Moors in Spain for her birthday or Christmas ('In memory of Granada and your dear Aunt Helen' was inscribed in Uncle Willa's copperplate hand on the fly-leaf), and another time Washington Irving's *Legends of the Alhambra*. When I was fourteen or fifteen, Uncle Willa had died long ago, my mother gave them both to me. I read Washington Irving's romantic compendium of travel, history and fairy tale; the study of Moorish art I had looked at with interest much earlier, in fact as soon as I could hold a book properly. It was an old monograph with wood engravings or, as the title page put it, 'illustrated with elegant photogravures'. Interleaved before the coloured plates, which gave off a peculiar smell, were protective sheets of soft, transparent paper on which the picture on the plate ('Panorama of the Alhambra and Sierra Nevada') was printed in outline with explanations so that, if you laid the transparent sheet over the coloured picture, you could read off what was the *torre de las damas* and what the *peinador de la reina*.

I grew up with the pictures of the Court of the Lions and

the Salon of the Abencerrages, with their horseshoe arches, slender columns, their *azulejo* tiles and gilded stalactites, without ever having seen them. I never thought of going there, although it's not that out of the way for us, not as far as away Peking or Tierra del Fuego. The idea of going to Granada, to *my* Granada, just never occurred to me. Did I think there was no point in going to see things that I had known so well since my earliest childhood? Was I afraid the reality would not match up to those 'elegant photogravures'?

My first trip to Granada needed this rather bizarre external impetus. Stephanie and I went by ourselves, Ferdi did not accompany us. I must admit that from the outset we arranged things so that we wouldn't have to take him with us. We said we'd had this silly idea. No one from our family had ever visited Aunt Helen's tomb, and after all, she was our mother's godmother. It was time, we said, to put that right, also in memory of our mother.

Naturally Stephanie made the suggestion as if she were assuming Ferdi would come along. As expected, he pulled a sour face, called it a lot of nonsense (what would he have said if he had known the real reason?) and declared his willingness to go to Carinthia, for example, where there were such lovely walks. He was afraid we would try to persuade him to agree to Granada and so made the suggestion himself that the two of us should go together. We waited until Easter was over and left on the Wednesday after Easter. Once we had decided on the trip Stephanie had no more dreams.

# VI

It was not difficult to find the small side street of the Escolastica, almost in the Antequeruela, the old Moorish quarter on the southern slopes of the Alhambra, in which was the Church of San Martín del Camarero, which is sometimes also called 'de la Yedra' because it used, before the rather dubious restoration of its façades, to be covered in ivy. 'Del Camarero' means 'of the waiter', so that initially I assumed it might be the guild church of the catering profession or something like that. But of course the designation was connected with the Dukes of I. who had their family vault here. The Dukes were hereditary chamberlains to Their Most Catholic Majesties, the kings of Castille and Leon, and 'camarero' also means 'chamberlain'.

San Martín, the ivy church, is not one of the famous churches of Granada. From the outside it appears to be a rather modest baroque church squeezed into the row of houses. That makes it look smaller than it actually is, so that when you go in the effect takes your breath away. You are in a huge space, dark, as are many Spanish churches. There were massive, almost ponderous pillars soaring upwards. The ceiling was lost in the darkness. The whole wall behind the altar was taken up with an over-large reredos, one of those almost violent works of sculpture made up of many smaller carvings. Gigantic, black, wrought-iron bars separated the altar-space from the rest of the church. The Spanish faith is a dark faith. Spanish Madonnas are as beautiful and cold as odalisques. Spanish Christs are always brutally maltreated victims, bleeding from more wounds than anywhere else in the world. As in most Spanish churches, the details of the golden reredos could not be made out. The flickering reflections of a row of large votive candles were playing over it, making the raised parts of the gilded relief glitter. There was an evil gleam in the old gold. I could imagine that Spanish churches put the fear of God into the Devil.

An old woman, swathed in a large, black, lace mantilla, was kneeling in one of the pews, a black rosary with beads of olive-wood slipping at a slow, regular rhythm through her fingers. We were treading quietly, but as we passed her, she looked up. Her flabby old face was covered in tears. Spain is a land of surprises – sometimes it is just as you imagined it.

A fat sacristan in a long, black overall unlocked the vault for us, after we had told him our aunt was buried there and given him a tip.

The vault was plain and bare. The ducal coffins, covered in unbelievable layers of dust, were distributed at random around it. In a side vault – we had to bend to enter – were some further coffins, twenty perhaps, crowded together and piled one on top of the other, as if in an undertaker's storeroom. The sacristan took an already pretty grubby handkerchief out of the incredibly deep pocket of his overall and began to dust the brass plates on the front of the coffins. The fifth or sixth was the one we were looking for. Engraved on it were the name and date of birth and death of our great-aunt, nothing else apart from a cross and three letters: R.I.P. – *requiescat in pace*.

The sacristan put away his handkerchief, sketched a bow, crossed himself and took one step backward, to allow us room for our reverence and grief. We didn't quite know what to do, so we just stood there for a while. Then Stephanie said, 'Requiescat in pace.' 'Amen', responded the sacristan. We all crossed ourselves. The sacristan shook us by the hand (which I found rather unsavoury, given that the proffered hand came from the depths of the pocket with the black handkerchief) and emitted a spate of words which were presumably belated condolences.

When we were back in the nave of the church I asked the sacristan what he knew of the grandees, the Dukes of I. The fact that I could not follow the whole of his lengthy answer probably lay not so much in the deficiencies in my knowledge of Spanish as in the fact that that he, as far as I could judge, spoke in a thick dialect and had a hare-lip into the bargain. As far as I could tell, he was giving us a compressed genealogy of the Dukes. The present Duke was called Fernando. (My later researches into the subject revealed that, as far as humanly possible, all the Dukes of I. were called Fernando.)

'How old is he?'

'His Highness was fifty-three on his last birthday', replied the sacristan. Assuming that the title had not gone to a collateral line, this 'Highness' must be one of Aunt Helen's former charges.

We learnt, however, that the Duke himself lived permanently in Madrid, so that the palace was as good as uninhabited. There was, of course, a caretaker in the Duke's service living there.

The palace – not so much what we would call a real palace as a large villa, a palatial stately home, patently an imitation of the Escorial – lay somewhat out of the town and to the north, close to the road leading to Jaén. We hired a small car from Hertz. Its appearance did not inspire great confidence in its reliability, but we assumed it would take us out to the palace and back without giving up the ghost. I certainly wouldn't have driven it along the Alpujarras.

It was midday, which can be as ghostly as midnight. It was very hot, summer weather by our standards. Even as we drove out of the town there was very little traffic apart from the odd dusty lorry. When we turned off to the right (the hotel porter had not only told us how to get there, but marked the route on the map, otherwise we would never have found it), our car was the only moving object as far as the eye could see. The air was quivering in the heat-haze and there was not a breath of wind, no birds singing or flying, only the constant chirping of the cicadas. On the seat next to me in the car Stephanie fell silent.

'Do you recognise the countryside?' I asked.

'I don't know', she said.

I had suggested we eat in Granada first and then drive out; I was sure it wouldn't be right to disturb the caretaker over lunch or during his siesta. But Stephanie was impatient. 'If we can't find the caretaker, we can always have a look a round; I'm sure there'll be somewhere to eat out there.'

There was nothing to look at and nowhere to eat.

All we could see of the palace was an endless expanse of yellowish wall shimmering in the heat, and a large, rusty wrought-iron gate that was locked. A group of small houses cowering in the sun a mile further on was like an abandoned settlement. Standing in the dusty street it was as if we were on another planet.

We drove on to the village, and in the hope that one of the houses might be an inn, we stopped and got out of the car. We found nothing and nobody, not even a donkey or a goat in the shadow of a tree, none of the miserable, clay-coloured Andalusian dogs, not a cat, not a hen.

'The best thing to do', I said, 'would be to go back to the town and drive back out again at four or five o'clock.'

Where the old man had come from, who suddenly appeared behind us and started talking to us, was a complete mystery to me. I started and spun round. Stephanie, who is normally much more nervous than I, turned calmly to face the man. And it was to her that the torrent of excited words gushing forth from the old man's lips was addressed. Even today I cannot believe I would not have heard him – an old man, lame and walking with a stick – if he had approached us by normal means. But it wasn't a ghost, as soon became obvious. Perhaps he had been hiding behind a fence or come out through a door we didn't notice.

Even more remarkable than the manner in which he materialised behind us was what he was saying, as far as we could understand it. It wasn't so much the fact that Stephanie and I only spoke what you might call gastronomic Spanish, sufficient for simple orders in restaurants, that made conversation with him difficult, as the almost complete absence of teeth in his mouth. Apart from his lack of teeth, the man did not give the impression of being poor. He was well-dressed, correctly dressed even, in a grey suit with a striped waistcoat, shoes polished until they shone and white spats. In his hand he carried a hard, flat hat, that restrained sombrero which in southern Spain old people still occasionally wear even on weekdays. The man had a patriarchal air, like a retired civil servant or lawyer.

He waved his hat in the air and went on talking. Stephanie looked at him, wide-eyed, and then she said to me, 'He takes me for Aunt Helen.'

The position of caretaker to the Dukes of I. was more or less hereditary, just as the Duke, for his part, was hereditary chamberlain to the King. The man, a genuine *caballero* as it turned out, who was much older than he looked, ninety-two, he said, was the former caretaker. The Duke had granted him a pension twenty years ago. As he, Señor Miguel Ridruejo y Sánchez, was unmarried, it was the son of his sister, his nephew Señor Miguel Alvaro Zardoja y Ridruejo, who had succeeded to the position. However, Señor Miguel Alvaro Zardoja y Ridruejo had died about ten years ago. His Highness' present caretaker was his grand-nephew, Señor Manuel Ramón Maria Zardoja y Dos Santos.

We responded with our, by comparison, relatively modest names.

Señor Ridruejo could remember Aunt Helen, '*la institutriz alemán*', very well. For a moment, he said, he had thought she was standing there in the flesh before him, so closely did Stephanie resemble her. He had thought, he said, that the dead were risen from their graves, that an apparition from the old days had come to visit him. Unfortunately my Spanish was not up to telling him that at first his sudden appearance had struck me as eerie too.

The old caretaker remembered the funeral. During the night after her death he had cried, he told us. Apart from that, the only occasion on which he had ever cried was the death of his mother, but when Aunt Helen, that wonderful woman, that beautiful woman, had died because of such a stupid accident, then he had cried. He remembered the man who had come from Germany, and he could also vaguely remember the young girl, our mother. But that was all a long time ago; the deep, dark years, he said, rolling, as far as he could without any teeth, the Spanish consonants with relish, the deep, dark years swallow up much sorrow and much joy, but more sorrow, he said, more sorrow . . .

It would, of course, be an honour, he went on, to show us the palace. It so happened that his grand-nephew, Señor Ramón Maria Zardoja y Dos Santos, was away on holiday with his family at the moment, but that did not matter. He didn't hold with these new-fangled ways; in all the years he had been in the Duke's service, it had never occurred to him to go away on holiday. But the Duke had approved the holiday. The things people got up to nowadays. God only knew where his grand nephew had gone to (with his wife and three children, Señora Rosa Maria Concepción Zardoja y Antequera and his great-grand-nephews, Miguel Fernando Francisco and Isidore Manuel Berenguér, as well as his great-grand-niece, Isabella Manuelita Maria de las Mercedes), to the seaside, he thought, as if there were anywhere more beautiful than here. It had certainly never occurred to him to go anywhere else. '*Quien no ha visto Granada, no ha visto nada.*'

We ushered Señor Ridruejo into our hired car. With his bad leg, he just about managed to squeeze into the front seat. I thought that he could have sat there quite normally if he had had the sense to get in – if you'll excuse the expression – rear-end first, but I could not say that in Spanish, certainly not with the required degree of politeness. So he insisted on sticking his stiff leg out of the door while we drove. For the short journey on these empty roads it was all right. As far as possible he kept the door pulled to with the handle of his walking stick. He did not need to go and fetch the key, he had it on him.

Stephanie grew quieter – no, she had been quiet the whole time, it was I who had had the difficult conversation with the old caretaker. She went tense, as if she was preparing herself inwardly for a difficult task. I didn't ask why.

We came to the rusted gate that we had already seen. Señor Ridruejo asked me to open it, as getting in and out of the car was so awkward for him. He took out a bunch of keys.

Whilst the caretaker was laboriously selecting the right

key, I could see Stephanie staring at the gate. It was a large, elaborate wrought-iron gate.

'Like the intertwined initials of some baroque prince', I said.

'Yes', said Stephanie, 'it's as if they were written in Indian ink on the green and brown of the garden behind.'

'Like the badge of an aristocratic theatre director on the patchwork costume of a clown playing a huntsman in a farce.'

'I think I've read that somewhere before', said Stephanie.

Señor Ridruejo had found the key and handed it to me on the ring. I got out and unlocked the gate. The hinges screeched and since, in the course of the centuries, the posts had presumably sunk, the bottom of the gate grated on the gravel as it dug a semicircle.

The palace itself we entered through a side door, through the steward's apartment. All we saw of it was the hall and a kind of kitchen-dining room: a festering ulcer of lower-middle-class lifestyle, consisting of mass-produced furniture and various plastic objects, had eaten its way into the baroque palace. It was as if the family of Señor Ridruejo's grand-nephew was doing its best to behave – here, under the noble arches of a princely seat – as if they were living in a block of flats. But perhaps that was the only way to stay sane in such a huge, empty house.

Señor Ridruejo showed us the two rooms which had been Aunt Helen's. Now they were standing empty, not just unoccupied, but empty, without furniture.

After the death of Aunt Helen – or Señorita Elena, as Señor Ridruejo called her – no one else had occupied them. It was Señor Ridruejo himself, who had been caretaker at the time, who had managed to arrange it so that the two room were left unoccupied. 'I couldn't have put up with seeing someone else going in and out of this door, or looking out of those windows.' It hadn't actually been very difficult to keep the two rooms locked up. In the first place, the palace had roughly two hundred other rooms, of which at most fifty percent were furnished, and secondly there had been no successor to Aunt Helen. The children of the then Duke had been almost completely grown up and after Aunt Helen's death no further governess had been appointed. It was, after all, to have been her last year in the Duke's service. 'The year after, she was going to get married', I said. 'I know', said the old man.

'A friend from her childhood days', I said.

'I met Herr Dr. S.', said the caretaker.

We stood around in the empty room, uncertain what to do. As a special favour, the caretaker opened the shutters. 'Those were her windows', he said.

Stephanie and I went to the window. A huge orange grove stretched all the way to the hills. I looked across at Stephanie. Did she recognise the garden? She did not return my look, but after a while she turned to Señor Ridruejo and said – they were the first words she had spoken since we had entered the palace –, 'And the room where it happened?'

The caretaker gave a faint nod, closed the shutters and led the way, dragging his bad leg, down a corridor to the right, then along one to the left.

'It was supposed', he said as he went, without turning round, 'to put the finishing touch to their education, the Viennese waltz. They were to learn the Viennese waltz – *el vals vienés.*'

At the end of the second corridor Señor Ridruejo opened a double door. We entered the drawing-room with the stone floor, the elaborate mosaic which looked like a flower garden. I thought I could hear Stephanie breathing a little more heavily. 'There', said the caretaker, pointing to a large, dark cabinet.

Stephanie looked around.

There was another thing, said the caretaker. He hobbled over to a sideboard and took something out. Then he went to another cabinet and opened that too. In it was a massive old gramophone with a horn. Señor Ridruejo wound it up.

'This is the waltz', he said, taking an old shellac record out of its wrapper. He put it on the gramophone and put the needle on. It took us a moment or two to get used to the scratching and wheezing, then we heard the croak of a palm-court orchestra playing '*Memories of Herkulesbad*'. '*Dreaming, I saw thee once more, true to the vows we both swore. Gone is all rapture with thee. Oh come back! Back to me . . .*' It was an adenoidal tenor. I would never have understood the text if I had not known it already. It was a song mother often used to sing.

'Can you understand what he's singing?' I asked Señor Ridruejo. The tenor was singing in German.

'No', he replied, 'I just feel it's sad.' He did not wait for the record to finish, switched the machine off, wrapped the record up again and put it back in the sideboard.

I was just about to try and translate the text for the caretaker when Stephanie pointed to the double doors at the other end of the room. 'What's behind that?'

He hobbled across to the door, his stiff leg dragging over the rich flower garden of stone. He opened the door. It led into a small, windowless vestibule. Without asking, Stephanie hurried past Señor Ridruejo and opened the next door. There she stopped.

'Would you . . . like to see the whole palace?' asked Señor Ridruejo.

'Let's go', said Stephanie. 'I'd like to leave now.'

When we were outside I gave Stephanie a questioning look. She sensed it, without looking at me. She nodded.

# VII

I have already mentioned that I am a bachelor, that I live alone. I am in the habit of spending Saturdays and Sundays, when everyone goes out to pollute the innocent meadows and shores of the lakes in our beautiful Highlands with their noise, in a room in my apartment which I call my 'winter garden'. At this moment I am writing my account of Stephanie's dreams in the 'winter garden'. In the months after our trip to Granada I immersed myself in a new passion which I will reveal in a moment, since it is connected with my sister's experiences.

On Saturday afternoons and Sundays it is marvellously quiet in the city. My 'winter garden', which in reality is a veranda which I have converted according to my own ideas and furnished somewhat more comfortably than usual, looks out onto a courtyard which on weekdays is full of noise, because some odious department store has its goods and suchlike delivered there. From one o'clock on Saturday onwards it is quiet.

I can see over the roofs of the city, and every stroke of the clocks in the old towers is clearly audible, even the splash of the little fountain in a wider stretch on one of the old streets behind the building opposite, which is drowned in the weekday roar.

It was on the 17th September of that year, not much after half past three. I was immersed in my papers. It had been a not particularly beautiful autumn day and the rays of an already pale sun were playing on the whorls of dust rising gently from my oleanders (my cleaning woman is not allowed to dust in the winter garden), when there was a ring at the door.

It was Ferdi, the last person I would have expected. I asked him in (not into the winter garden, that is sacred, but into the living room), offered him a seat and asked if I could get him anything to drink.

'No, thank you', he said. 'Stephanie's gone.'

'How do you mean, gone?' I asked.

At the beginning of this account I mentioned how a fairly rudimentary personality can be ennobled, so to speak, by suffering. Even now, as he sat facing me, he showed dignity, there's no other word for it. He had by then got over the initial, paralysing shock. Now he was doing what was necessary, or rather, what it was in his power to do. He went about it with a quiet conscientiousness.

'I don't know either', he said. 'I don't know why, I don't know where. I don't even know exactly when. She hasn't been to see you?'

He asked the question almost timidly, as if he had no hope the answer would be in the affirmative. I merely shook my head.

'You don't know when?' I asked.

'It's very strange', he said. 'She wasn't there when I woke up this morning. I have informed . . .' – he took a deep breath, as if he were about to lift a heavy load – '. . . the police. Around noon.'

'And yesterday evening?'

'Yesterday evening we went to bed as usual.'

'And you noticed nothing during the night?'

'No.'

At this point I think I ought to mention that, however much, in the first instance, I was shaken by Ferdi's news, I was not surprised by it. I did not let it show. Even after our trip to Spain, Stephanie and I had not told Ferdi anything about her dreams and the things connected with them. The dreams had returned, at longer or shorter intervals, though without any pattern we could discern, at least not at the time. They were becoming a torment for Stephanie. Every night was like a horrible dragon approaching, and the fear only left her in the early morning when she woke without having dreamt, or only after other, harmless dreams. But by the late morning the fear of what the coming night might bring was starting to creep up on her, and the fear was stronger, the farther back the last dream lay. What neither of us realised at the time was that it was in Stephanie's hands, literally in her hands, whether she 'dreamt' or not.

She pretended to be suffering from insomnia, spent whole nights reading, lost weight and became irritable, tormenting everyone around her. It even came to a quarrel between us, between Stephanie and me – I think it must have been the first quarrel between us in our whole lives – when I told her it couldn't go on like that, she ought to be honest with Ferdi and go to see a neurologist. She accused me of believing she was mad and said no doctor, whether a specialist in nerves or anything else, could help her.

It goes without saying that Ferdi could not fail to notice the change in Stephanie. He was, there is no other way of putting it, a model of consideration. Nor did he fail to realise that the change in Stephanie had started after our return from Spain. He came to his own – that is the natural – conclusion about the matter, though no one can blame him for that. No one should blame anyone for assuming the obvious, in most cases it is the obvious explanations that apply, rather than supposedly more profound ones.

Ferdi assumed, or was afraid, that since our trip to Spain there was 'another man' in Stephanie's life.

'You mean', I said, 'that she's . . . fallen in love?'

Ferdi said nothing.

'. . . is having an affair?'

'No', Ferdi replied quickly, 'definitely not. I'm not so stupid that I wouldn't have noticed something like that.'

'Did you . . .'

'Yes. It's not the kind of thing one ought to do, but I had my suspicions and I wanted to know what was going on.'

'You employed someone to keep an eye on her?'

'Yes.'

'No', I said, 'one can't take exception to that.'

'I now know', said Ferdi, 'that she has not been guilty of the least infidelity. Except, perhaps, in her mind. I couldn't keep that under surveillance.'

'So to put it bluntly', I said, 'you think that Stephanie has fallen in love but because she's a decent person, she has not started an affair, and the unhappy love has driven her insane, more or less? If that's the case, why has she run off then?'

'Please tell me', said Ferdi, 'whether anything happened while you were in Spain.'

At that moment, seeing a big strong man like Ferdi actually appearing to shrink physically as he slumped into his chair in childlike bewilderment – which he bore manfully enough, it must be said – I wondered whether I shouldn't tell him all about the dreams. However, he interrupted the train of thought.

'There are other inexplicable things as well', he said. The moment he could concentrate on ordinary, concrete details, he sat up straight. 'For example, this morning the front door was locked, the chain was on, and the key was in the lock on the inside.'

'But your house has a door into the garden, doesn't it?'

'That was locked from the inside, too. That door can only be locked from the inside.'

'Through the window?'

'There was a window open upstairs, only upstairs, our bedroom window, but then she would have had to have jumped from the first floor. There's a flower-bed underneath; there would have been marks. Anyway, I would have woken up. She hasn't taken any money, nor her passport, nothing.'

'Which clothes?'

'I've had a look. I couldn't say for sure that there's nothing at all missing, no dress or blouse, skirt or trousers gone. I'd have to have a complete list in my head. But she didn't wear a coat. She's got four, that I do know, and all four are there, her fur coat, a short one, more of a jacket, a raincoat and another raincoat.'

I said nothing. Ferdi was thinking.

'She left her wedding ring', Ferdi went on. 'but she took the other ring with her, the ring I gave her as a present on our wedding anniversary.'

I had suspected that this ring might play some part in the affair ever since we, that is, Stephanie and I, had said goodbye to Señor Ridruejo, the caretaker of the palace near Granada. We had thanked him for showing us the palace, though he could not know the significance it had for us. Señor Ridruejo, the complete *caballero*, had refused to accept our thanks (not to mention a tip); on the contrary, he said, it was *he* who should be thanking *us*. Fate had been kind enough to let him see once more in the *Señora* – he gave a little bow in Stephanie's direction – the living image of Doña Elena. He kissed Stephanie's hand, then gave a gasp of astonishment.

What was the matter, I asked.

Nothing, he said, only the ring, the coat of arms on the ring was the coat of arms of the Dukes of I.

Of course, I should have seen the connection immediately, but brilliant intuition only works in retrospect. Perhaps my attention was drawn away from the real significance of the ring by Stephanie's remark that henceforward she would wear it with special pleasure. Stephanie did not wear the ring all the time, not even after that, and for a very simple reason: the metal chafed her fingers; every ring chafed her skin, even her wedding ring, and if she wore one for too long she would get tiny blisters under it, a harmless, but not particularly pleasant condition.

That very same evening in the Washington Irving Hotel, a charming, old-fashioned place beside the Alhambra and far from the noise of the city – we had taken rooms there on the recommendation of a friend of mine, an expert on Moorish Spain, thus avoiding those booming concrete hangars like the Luz Granada – that very same evening I subjected the ring to a long and close examination. The coat of arms meant nothing to me, I'm not interested in heraldry, but presumably it was the arms of the Dukes of I.; Ridruejo would know the arms of his lord and master. But in the flourish at the bottom I thought I could make out an S. and an I. Now those are also Stephanie's initials. Later on Stephanie asked her husband whether it was because of the initials that he had bought the ring, but Ferdi had not even noticed them, he thought they were just part of the scroll-work. He had bought the ring from a jeweller in D–straße who knew about old jewelry and occasionally had that kind of thing in stock.

We sat together in my sitting room for a while longer, Ferdi and I, trying to work out what we could do, but naturally nothing occurred to us. I offered Ferdi a bed for the night, so that he wouldn't have to sleep alone in that house all that way out of town, but he refused. He preferred to be at home, he said; the last thing he wanted was for Stephanie, if708; she should return – and God grant that she would – to find herself locked out of the house. She had not taken her key.

When Ferdi left it was about seven o'clock. I did not go back to the winter garden and the papers connected with my new passion, but changed and went out for dinner in *The Greenroom*, as I did almost every evening.

# VIII

After we had stayed for a few days in Granada, during the late spring of that year, we spent a further fortnight in Spain, going on to Seville and Cordoba, even though Stephanie was no longer in the mood for sightseeing. Once she said, 'It's like a black cloud hanging over my head that I can't escape, now that I know it's not a dream after all, but some kind of reality. It's as if I'd been told I had cancer. But since we're here, we might as well go to Cordoba and Seville.'

Immediately after our return I began to look into the history of the Dukes of I. The family, although not one of the very oldest, had many links with the history of Spain. Especially during the two centuries of Spain's greatness – the 16th and 17th centuries – it had produced generals and ministers, one or two bishops and cardinals as well, and even a canonised saint; naturally it was connected with all the other great families of Spain, and also with some noble families in France, Italy and South Germany. In the 18th century history has much less to say about their exploits. Apart from an admiral at the beginning of the century the family produced no more notable personalities. Even the admiral was distinguished by the fact that he never succeeded in winning a naval battle. The poet, Ignacio de I., was only the son of a lady's maid of one of the duchesses who took the name of his patron with the Duke's permission. I suspect, however, that he was a bastard of the ducal line.

The only monograph that I came across in connection with the family dealt with with two statesmen among them, a Don Fernando de I., 5th Duque, who was a minister under Philip III, and a Don Francisco de I. – a younger son of the 5th Duque – who was ambassador to London and Vienna, and later minister under Philip III. The ancestors and descendants of these two grandees were only mentioned in the introductory chapters or, in the case of the latter, the afterword.

The family tree that was appended was incomplete, I had to reconstruct the ancestral line of the Dukes of I. from the genealogies of related families. It was a painstaking task piecing together the mosaic. I immersed myself more and more in the material, and before I knew what had happened genealogy, that science that was once so important and is now merely a by-way of history, had become my new passion. My attempt to go straight to the source produced little in the way of results; the letter I wrote to the present Duque in Madrid, asking whether there was a family archive which could provide me with information on certain genealogical questions, remained unanswered. More productive on the other hand, was my correspondence with a man I had come across professionally some years ago and whom, now that I had taken up genealogy, I managed with some difficulty to trace in order to ask his advice: Dr. Nikolaus von Colleoni, a descendant of the great *condottiere*, in which distant relationship he would show a charmingly diffident pride. Every time we passed it, he would stand below Verrocchio's equestrian statue of his ancestor and ask, apparently or genuinely forgetting that it was a joke he had already made several times, 'A family likeness? No? Pity.'

As a kind of sideline, Dr. von Colleoni was head of the private archive of a princely house, but his main claim to fame was for his intimate knowledge of the most intricate ramifications of the family trees of all the noble families of Europe. The House of Habsburg was his speciality. I think that whenever he closed his eyes the genealogy of this great dynasty must have appeared in permanent letters of fire before his mind's eye. Whether you asked him about Emperor Rudolf I, Maximilian II or Emperor Franz Josef, he could immediately count off on his fingers the whole horde of their children, with each and every Christian name and nickname, right down to the very last Nepomuk Salvator; he could even list all the miscarriages and still-births of the least-favoured of the archduchesses, by which time his genealogical knowledge already had a touch of the gynaecological.

Dr. von Colleoni pursued my inquiries with gusto. He

copied family trees for me, made excerpts from archives, sent me books and gave me references to books which I could get through our own State Library.

My 'new passion', as I called it (by now it has died down again, I have to say) was thus a by-product of the question of what happened to the line of the Spanish Dukes of I. in the 18th century. Genealogically speaking I had long since outgrown them, in the shade of the oleanders on the walls of my winter garden were the family trees of ancient Burgundian lairds, the Lombard Princes of Spoleto, and Armenian kings, and my correspondence with Dr. von Colleoni was dealing with delicate questions of relationships among the old Dukes of Brittany, or the extremely tangled genealogy of the *Wild und Raugraf* from the Nahe region, when I came across something that made me prick up my ears. It was an essay in an old specialist periodical that happened to mention, as I already knew, that the older line of the Dukes of I. died out in the year 1761 with the IX Duque, who was called Fernando, what else? The ninth Duke had neither children nor brothers or sisters, and his father had only had sisters. The title went, strictly in accordance with Salic Law, to the next agnate, now the X Duque, who was naturally another Fernando and who was, incidentally the grandson of the above-mentioned luckless admiral. There was no problem with the succession to the title, but a lawsuit broke out over certain estates the IX Duque had inherited from his mother's side and to which the tenth Duke, the distant relative, now made a claim which was disputed by other relatives. The case dragged on, outliving the tenth Duke, and the parties only reached a settlement during the time of his son, the eleventh Duke who, exceptionally, was not called Fernando but Carlos Luis. One of the important aspects in the case was the fact that the ninth Duke, the one who had no children to succeed to the title, had died in strange circumstances. It was also odd that the widow of the Duke – she was called Estefanía and was considerably younger than he – laid no claim at all to these estates.

In the appendix to this article was a copy of a laconic

document. Dr. von Colleoni, whom I naturally consulted on the matter, thought that, reading between the lines, it implied the Duke had been murdered. Every attempt appeared to have been made to render the account of the circumstances as unclear as possible, presumably to avoid a scandal. He had been unable, wrote the author, to establish what had subsequently happened to the Duchess. What was certain was that after her husband's death she had not lived on one of the I. family estates, nor on any of the estates of her own family. The author had gone to the trouble of examining the register of every Spanish convent to which ladies of the nobility might retire. None of them recorded an Estefanía de I. As far as history was concerned, the lady had vanished from the face of the earth.

Had she murdered her husband?

Dr. von Colleoni thought it was not beyond the bounds of possibility. Such things, he said, happened in the best of families. Especially in the best of families, he added after some reflection.

# IX

I am afraid the previous chapter, in which I was concerned to reflect a certain inner development of my own understanding of this sad affair, may have confused the sequence of the actual events somewhat. My genealogical studies stretched over years, and I only came across the article I mentioned after Stephanie had returned. Yes, she did return. But that was almost worse than her disappearance.

During those weeks after the Easter we spent in Spain Stephanie did not dream at all. It was, although I could not say why, precisely what I had expected. Afterwards she started dreaming again, with great frequency but irregularly, as I mentioned before. The dreams became a torment which took her to the brink to madness. I often asked her what her 'dreams' were like, whether they were different from before, whether she saw different things. No, she said, they were always the same. She didn't like talking about them, often she would even lose her temper. In spite of that, sometimes I couldn't stop myself pressing her with questions. Had she got out of bed again 'over there'? No, she said, she wouldn't dream of getting out of bed again.

Shortly before the 17th September, that is just before the night she disappeared, she was in a more approachable mood. It was at the beginning of the week, the 12th or 13th, and it was the last time I saw her before her disappearance. I asked her how she knew the man in the other bed was dead? As always, whatever happened, Stephanie's hands were busy; she let her knitting sink to her lap and looked up.

'Because he . . .', she said, 'because he . . . his throat was cut. I hope you never have to see anything like that. It was as if . . .'

'As if . . .?'

'As if he had a bloody mouth, a second mouth without lips, wide, sharp, gaping from his neck. The cut was deep; his head was lolling back in the pillows and his eyes were open and glassy. The whole bed was full of blood. That's how I knew he was dead. Are you satisfied now?'

I asked no more questions. She was already speaking in an irritated tone. It was immediately after that short conversation that I decided not to ask any more questions at all, not because there were not things I would still like to know, but because the thought occurred to me that it was perhaps not so much the talking about it that she disliked as the being asked. Perhaps she would tell me all the more, the less I said about it, just like the hero in Hauptmann's story *The Heretic of Soana*, who fled when anyone asked him a question and whom the narrator provoked into telling his life story by the ploy of just sitting beside him without saying a word. Whether that would have worked with Stephanie I can't say; I only had that one afternoon to sit beside her in silence.

We were sitting out on the patio. Stephanie had made a pot of coffee. As she brought out the coffee things on a round, red tray with a light-coloured linen napkin on it, she quoted one of our mother's maxims – she still laughed occasionally –, 'The best coffee can be spoilt by water.' I answered with another of mother's adages concerning coffee, 'A good cup of coffee is one you can turn upside down without it running out.'

Stephanie had also brought out a large black shawl that she wrapped round her shoulders. I had bought it for her in the spring in Cordoba, a large, triangular shawl with long fringes, a *mantón* the Spanish women wear.

'Does it keep you warm?' I asked.

She nodded.

Summer was over. The air was clear. The leaves of a small birch tree in Stephanie's garden were quivering in a breeze so gentle only the birch leaves felt it. The tiny autumn midges were swirling round like a cloud of dust over a bed in which the roses had already been pruned back. There seemed to be a slight hint of woodsmoke in the air, but it was probably only the dry odour of the soil; perhaps, even, we were just imagining it because it belongs to our image of autumn. The

Virginia creeper that grew around the outdoor seat had already changed colour. A larch – behind the birch, it was already in the neighbour's garden – stood out like an orange flame among the dark green shrubs, as if it was drawing the light of the sun towards it like a prism. A tiny spider let itself down on an invisible thread to within a couple of inches above the table. Stephanie looked up from her knitting and watched the spider. The spider paused then quickly hauled itself back up its thread into the Virginia creeper. It was Stephanie's last autumn.

The year followed its course, the winter when Stephanie was no longer there, the Christmas I spent with Ferdi. He asked me to. It was awful for him to have to spend Christmas Eve in his house, but he was still afraid Stephanie might return home unannounced and find the door locked; Christmas Eve might just be the time she would come home. I was the only one among his relatives who lived alone and therefore had nothing to do on Christmas Eve, so Ferdi invited me to keep him company. I stayed until Boxing Day. It was, as might be expected, terrible. Ferdi had put up a Christmas tree, had decorated it and made a meal for the two of us. And naturally he had bought a present for Stephanie, a silk blouse. He had a present for me, too. I had expected that, feared it even, since, as I have implied several times, we had hardly anything in common at all. But that evening I had to admire both his taste and his tact. He had put in some real detective work to find one of my best friends, whom he had met briefly at my apartment, and asked him for advice. I had once mentioned to this friend that I would quite like a small clock for the table in my study. There are things like that, things you would love to have but never buy for yourself.

Ferdi gave me a small antique clock under a glass cover. 'I chose the one with the quietest tick', he said. 'You can hardly hear it at all; just on the hour there's a little chime.' Originally I had meant to suggest to Ferdi that I would come, but that we should not bother giving each other presents. I realised, however, that he wanted a 'proper' Christmas, so I had to rack my brains to think of a present for him. Nothing occurred to me, so I gave him something that was really a present for Stephanie. I had purchased two engravings at an auction in November, two good Piranesis. I had one framed in a style Stephanie would like. It represented an old mooring place, long since disappeared, on the Tiber near the Palazzo Borghese. I was astonished that Ferdi could appreciate it, which was apparent from a couple of far from stupid remarks he made as he looked at the picture.

In spite of that it was, of course, an awful evening. It was painfully obvious that Ferdi was waiting.

Around seven o'clock he lit the candles on the tree. Unfortunately, he also put on a record of the Christmas carols I hate so much. I said nothing. Perhaps it was all part of his idea of Christmas Eve, and anyway, I was just happy that he did not ask me to sing along.

At half past seven he went into the kitchen to get the meal. After dinner he opened the bottle of '59 *Juliusspital* I had brought (not to be had for love nor money nowadays).

'Will the blouse be the right size for Stephanie?' he asked.

I said nothing. He was asking quite a different question. What he really meant was, 'Where do you think she is?' Once again I was close to telling him the whole story. Perhaps I should have, although it would probably have made no difference at all to the way things turned out and would have been no help either to him or to Stephanie. But why didn't I tell him? There were many reasons, some, I must admit, confused and unclear to myself, but the main one was to avoid the reproachful question of why I hadn't told him all that before?

But I did stand up and tell him the truth. 'Ferdi', I said, 'don't ask me why I know, but Stephanie is alive.'

Ferdi remained seated and looked up at me. 'Is there something you know? I mean something more precise?'

'No', I replied, and there I was back with the lie, even if only a half lie, 'no, I'm just sure she's alive.'

'Will she come back?'

I thought for a moment, sat down again.

'I'm inclined to think', I said, 'that she will come back.'

She did come back. During the very cold night of the first to the second of January she was standing on the patio, frozen stiff and dressed only in a thin, cambric nightdress with a light woollen wrap over it, her bare feet in open slippers. She knocked on the roller-shutters. Ferdi, who always went to his office very early because the drivers had to be sent off, was already awake. It was half past five.

Stephanie did not respond to anything he said. He put her to bed and called the doctor. The doctor could find nothing wrong, but to be on the safe side he had her taken into hospital. At eight o'clock, Ferdi told me what had happened, and around midday I went to see her in hospital. She was awake but completely oblivious to the world around. She did not seem to recognise anyone. I asked to be left alone with her for a few minutes. I was hoping she was merely pretending to have suffered a blackout. 'Stephanie', I said, 'I haven't told anyone . . .'

She turned her face towards me, but the expression on it was completely blank.

After a few days she was transferred from the hospital to a psychiatric unit. I took her hand. It was ice-cold. She was wearing the ring.

I visited her there several times, eight in all; the first three visits were in quick succession, at intervals of a few days after she had been admitted, then one in the middle of February, when she was confined to bed once more, and four times in March, in her last week, the last time on the day – it was a Thursday – on the evening of which she died. During the first visits, and during the one in February, she was as dead to the world as on that first day, not responding and clearly not remembering anything. In the last week, as her physical condition deteriorated rapidly, she showed signs of recognition.

On the last day, she spoke.

# X

The visits to the psychiatric hospital were torture. Is there anyone who can bear another person's suffering? Only someone who lacks awareness. Can anyone be aware and still bear the sight of human suffering? Only if they are strong and active enough to be able to help. Someone like myself, whose profession is concerned with theoretical matters, with, if you like, the aesthetic (and useless) aspects of this world, feels, when confronted with suffering, superfluous and even harmful, and all those great and beautiful things around which my life usually revolves come to seem like frippery.

The psychiatric hospital is situated in a town well away from the city. In the past, even when I was still at school, the town was so small that half of it seemed to consist of the huge expanse of the hospital with its countless large and small buildings surrounded by a high wall. Of course, that wasn't really the case, the town was twenty times (today more) the size of the hospital. The main thing was that there was nothing else of any significance in the town, so that the name of the mental institution was coupled with that of the town, the significance of the institution absorbed that of the town, so that not only was the town equated with the institution, it completely disappeared behind it. For the whole region, the name of the town meant the mental institution and the mental institution alone. To go to that town, or to come from it, was synonymous with being a lunatic. Today the town has grown enormously and has recovered from its role as a term of abuse. But I am old enough to have suffered from it. I was born in the place. As long as I was at primary school it didn't matter, because all the other pupils came from the town, but things were bad when I went to the *Gymnasium* in the city and was exposed to the teasing of my classmates. We left when I was about fourteen; never in my life have I been more relieved. All that is probably the reason why I never felt at home there.

Of course, as a child I never entered the psychiatric hospital – the lunatic asylum as its less politically correct but probably more precise designation was at the time. The attitude of the grown-ups infected the children: we repressed all consciousness of the asylum, denied its existence. The headmaster of the primary school once wrote a study, which was published at the cost of the parish council, in which he drew on old documents to prove that historically the area beyond where the railway line now ran, that is the grounds on which the asylum stood, actually belonged to the neighbouring parish.

Nevertheless, there were of course connections. The children of the hospital staff, of the doctors, teachers and nurses, went to our school. They told the most horrifying stories. The son of the asylum janitor even lived inside the great wall. He told us there was a ward in which lunatics without arms and legs lived. They crawled around like snakes, he said. It was an image that plagued me for years, sometimes it suddenly flashes into my mind even today.

Just like the grown-ups when they went for a walk, we avoided going near the institution when we were out playing, as if the very proximity were infectious.

Thus those sad and pointless visits to see Stephanie were a kind of return for me. The streets were covered with snow that had been pounded into filthy, muddy slush by hundreds of feet and wheels. Bare trees stood in greenish-brown meadows, the beeches still with the shrivelled leaves from the previous year. The sky stretching over the flat landscape was always a pallid yellow or grey. Usually it was raining. From January to March the weather did not improve at all.

Stephanie was in a building where they housed all those who were physically as well as mentally ill, a general hospital within the institution. There were advantages in that, the clinical atmosphere anaesthetised the sense of being in a lunatic asylum. The disadvantage was that it was at the far end of the grounds, so that visitors had to pass through the whole of the mental institution. Spitting or waving from the windows were giggling spectres, pale, fat creatures who had remained in a kind of larval stage; on the paths you encountered sexless, ageless beings, lips trembling, arms dangling, eyes staring, all dressed in the dismal institution uniform. Sometimes one of them would run along beside you, constantly raising the hat that was possibly his only private possession. 'No need to be afraid', said the male nurse, 'he wouldn't harm a fly.'

Clouds of steam reeking of cheap cooking fat wafted from the kitchens. The corridors, too, gave off a greasy, rancid smell. I always hurried through them, looking neither to the right nor to the left, never taking in anything more than was absolutely necessary, and even that was more than enough for me. I met deranged children who were being taken for a walk, tied together with a long piece of string; I met an old, bald woman who was trying to suckle a grubby doll; I met a creature as fat as a barrel with its arms sticking out at the side like flippers – it was sitting on a stone under a tree, singing; once a young woman whose face was a patchwork of burns, slipped me a note. There were stars drawn on it with an incomprehensible message of unreadable or meaningless words scattered among them. I gave it to the doctor, but he threw it into the waste-paper basket.

There was one thing that did surprise me: the ones that looked the craziest were the doctors. The doctor who was treating Stephanie had a squint and – this was very unusual for 1961 – a long, shaggy mane; all the time he was talking he used to jiggle around in his chair. He had the habit – it seemed to be compulsive – of quickly repeating the last word of anything he said in a quiet voice. ('Tell me', he asked me as soon as we met, 'can you explain why your sister always speaks Spanish when she wakes up – up?') But he was a good doctor, a sensible man, and I have good reason to think that he did everything he could, if not to help Stephanie, by that time she was beyond help, a least not to torment her.

His superior, a consultant who also taught at the university, always wore a brown beret with his white coat, and used to bark instead of knocking at doors. The assistant, a young man, had a very long beard, which he usually wore braided in two plaits. Whenever I saw him, he was invariably chewing a pickled gherkin, a supply of which he carried around loose in the pocket of his white coat, which naturally had damp patches.

'Even I don't know where we get it from – from', said the doctor with the squint. 'Does dealing with the insane slowly drive us insane, or is it only people who are already partly mentally disturbed who are interested in psychiatry – psychiatry?'

In all, I visited Stephanie eight times in the three months before her death. That isn't very often. The one thing I can say for myself is that it wasn't the effort it cost me every time just to enter the sanatorium, with its smell of cheap floor polish and urine, that stopped me visiting her more frequently, but Stephanie's condition. I sat by her bedside and looked at her. She stared past me, or looked at me out of unfamiliar eyes, sometimes even with fear in them. Often she would cry when I addressed a cautious remark to her. So I usually sat there in silence. After ten minutes – ten minutes is a very long time – I would start to feel foolish. I won't deny that sometimes I felt something like anger, only: anger at whom? At what? But I couldn't just get up and leave after only ten minutes. You drive out in the rain and snow, half an hour there and half an hour back, you have to stay longer than ten minutes. I caught my thoughts slipping off along strange byways, just as they do when you are listening to a badly delivered sermon or some boring music. I would round my thoughts up again, but at best I would sit beside Stephanie's bed pondering on my collection of memories, as if I were beside her grave. The visits were an irksome duty and a pointless waste of time into the bargain. I swear, if Stephanie had given the slightest sign of recognition, I would have gone to see her every day.

In the third week of March the doctor with the squint told me it would not be long now – now. He explained Stephanie's physical illness to me, a particularly insidious form of cancer of the bone marrow which must have been present within her for a long time; it was incurable anyway, but her baffling mental illness rendered her case completely hopeless. The daily blood transfusions were no longer making any difference, and by the end Stephanie was hooked up to the plasma bottle day and night as if it were a water-tap left permanently running.

In those last two weeks I drove out four times. My visits were to the doctor rather than to my sister, but of course there was nothing new he could tell me. At this point I again wondered whether I should not tell the doctor the whole story. I decided against it when he said that even if we had known what her mental illness was, there was nothing we could do to help her any more – more. Not any more – any more. At an earlier stage, perhaps. (I really admired him for suppressing his silly quirk of repeating the last word of every sentence for that 'perhaps', that 'perhaps' alone.) As things were, it was best that I had not told him anything.

Stephanie died on the night of the thirtieth of March. I visited her for the last time on the thirtieth of March, at four o'clock in the afternoon. It was a horrible, rainy day typical of early spring – or, better, the end of winter. It was damp and cold, the rain was mixed with snow. It was one of those days when you wonder whether there will ever be fine weather anywhere in the world again. My shoes were sodden and my trousers soaked to the knees.

The doctor with the squint was not there. As soon as I reached the ward one of the male nurses told me Stephanie had 'woken up'. Without any medical knowledge at all, I suspected that this was not a sign that gave grounds for hope, quite the contrary.

Stephanie was very weak. As always during those last few days she looked as if she were trussed up in the tangle of tubes through which the blood was being pumped into her body. She gave me a smile.

'Have you told them anything at all?' she asked.
'Of your story?' I said.
'You haven't told anyone, I hope?'
I was happy I could deny it with a clear conscience
'You were . . . there?' I said.

'Of course', she replied.

I was wondering whether I should ask her any more questions. 'Don't ask me anything now', she said, 'I wouldn't be able to talk for very long, anyway.'

She was silent. What could I say in such a situation? How much did she know of her condition?

'I'm not going to take it with me when I go. You'll find it.'

'I'll find what?'

'The letter. I've written you a letter. I've buried it. A long letter. A notebook. A blue notebook. I buried it in a jewelry casket. I couldn't bring the casket back with me.'

'Where did you bury it?'

'There, of course', she said. 'Over there. A jewelry casket that belonged to the Duchess, that is, to me . . .'

She was silent, she had to gather her strength again. After a while she went on, 'You'll find it. It won't be difficult for you. You see, I knew what changes would be made around the palace, I'd already been there two hundred years later; it was before that, do you understand? I knew where nothing would be changed. That's where I buried the jewelry casket with the notebook. We drove in through the gate with the old caretaker. You remember?'

'Naturally.'

'Beyond the gate there's a line of old trees, *then* they were quite small. It's between the second and the third tree, half way between, exactly half way. You'll have to measure it. I dug very deep, at least three feet. I know that's not really very deep, it was as deep as I could manage. I did the digging myself. I couldn't mention it to anyone. The day before, I stole the spade from the gardener. I hope he didn't notice.'

'And what's in this exercise book?'

'Don't ask me now', she said in a very soft voice. 'Everything's in it. They were about to come to fetch me.'

'Who?'

'It's all in there. The next day. I had to leave and I couldn't take anything with me . . .'

Then the doctor with the squint finally did arrive. Outside, I asked him whether it was a good sign that Stephanie had recovered consciousness, if you could call it that. He made a gesture which could mean yes and could mean no. I've often seen doctors make it. It's impossible to describe, it consists of all the significant expressions and meaningful gestures, which the average patient associates with doctors, brought together and compressed into a fraction of a second. I assume that this extremely taxing piece of dumb show is taught at a special seminar for advanced medical students. I further assume that there is a school of thought among some eminent physicians which considers mastery of this subtle grimace to be more important than a practical acquaintance with matters of physiology and anatomy.

The next day, at six o'clock in the morning, Ferdi rang me up to tell me that Stephanie had died during the night.

# XI

Professional obligations prevented me from leaving immediately after Stephanie's death for the place where, according to her last words, I would find the letter or message that she had deposited for me.

There is no need for me to say that never for one moment did I doubt the real, objective truth of my sister's last words, just as there is no need for me to say that I did not breathe a word of what she had told me to anyone, least of all to Ferdi.

It was only the weekend following the weekend after Stephanie's death that I managed to free myself from my professional obligations, for three days, from midday on Friday to Tuesday morning. The days I had to spend waiting until I was free to fly to Granada were a torment. I was obsessed with the idea that just at that moment something might be happening over there. In my mind's eye I saw workmen felling the trees, laying electricity cables, I saw diggers tearing up the earth. But there was no help for it, I had to wait those two weeks. It was not made any better by the terrible air connections to Granada. I only arrived late on Friday evening. I couldn't really do anything at that time of night, but I did do something: I took a taxi and drove out to the palace to peer through the wrought-iron gate. The trees were still there, and no diggers. Relieved, I drove back to the hotel. The taxi-driver thought I was mad.

The next morning, Saturday, I took a taxi again. I was counting on being able to confide my secret (suitably doctored, of course) to the old caretaker, Señor Ridruejo. I had a plausible story ready, but there was one thing I had left out of my calculations. His nephew, the reigning caretaker, so to speak, was there, and in his presence the old man was as good as unapproachable.

The old man sat there in his one-storey house, his stiff leg stuck out in front of him, and negotiated with me through the door. He would not let me in and had no intention of coming out. Whether he was just pretending to have difficulty understanding my Spanish or whether he really didn't remember me, I could not tell. What did surprise me was that he behaved as if the name of my great-aunt meant nothing to him, when he had almost been in tears when we had talked to him before. The only explanation I have been able to come up with was that the previous time, when his nephew was away and the old man was deputising for him, he must have exceeded his authority, which had led to a disagreement between uncle and nephew. Perhaps there had been no love lost between them even before that.

But what could it have been that made it such a heinous overstepping of the mark? That he had allowed strangers into the palace at all? Or showing us the record? Whatever it was, the way the old man behaved warned me not to mention the friendly reception we had been accorded the previous year to his nephew. For the moment there was nothing to be done

In order to remain as close to the truth as possible without having go off on tortuous explanations which – particularly given the linguistic difficulties – I could not expect anyone to believe, I had worked out a reasonably plausible story: Great-aunt Helen had lived in the the palace, she had even died there. It had always been known in the family that she had kept a diary, but we had assumed it had been lost. Only now, following certain letters which had been found among my sister's effects – letters from my grandmother to my mother – had we discovered that the diary had been buried at such and such a spot in the garden of the palace. Might I please be permitted to dig it up? I had brought a small spade with me from home.

The caretaker – the nephew, Señor Ridruejo junior – listened to my story (I had rehearsed it in Spanish) and then said the palace was the private estate of the Dukes of I. and was not open to visitors. I repeated the story I had learnt in Spanish, but again the caretaker did not seem to understand. I pointed to my spade. Comprehension flooded the eyes of the caretaker. Was I *un botánico* then? Did I want to dig for *orugas*? What are *orugas*? I looked it up in my dictionary: *la oruga* – the caterpillar.

I hesitated briefly. Should I change tack? From my great-aunt's diary to *unas orugas*? Had I been sure he would have let me go and hunt caterpillars in the garden alone, I would have risked it and invested a few pesetas in a tip. But what if he should accompany me and discover that instead of a botanical caterpillar I dug up Stephanie's papers? If I had gone about it the wrong way, I might have blocked the only legal route by which I could most easily get at the letter.

So I denied all knowledge of *orugas* and packed my spade back into my bag. However, what I did learn from the caretaker was that the Dukes had a steward who lived in Granada, a lawyer called Dr. Gonsalvo Mitón. I even got his address.

I went back to Granada, asking the taxi-driver to take me straight to Dr. Mitón's chambers. The building was on the Plaza Nueva, close to the beginning of the steep alley that leads up to the Alhambra. By that time it was midday on Saturday. Dr. Mitón's chambers were closed. A goitrous old concierge in a black housecoat was sweeping the entrance to the block of offices with a broom that had hardly any bristles left. I asked her whether Dr. Mitón might be available at home to deal with urgent cases. She had no idea. There was also a shoe shop in the building which the owner was just closing. I asked him if he knew where Dr. Mitón lived, but he did not know either. In order to leave no stone unturned, I went to the Central Post Office, where they had not only telephone kiosks but also telephone books. Under Dr. Mitón was only his office number. I tried it, but naturally no one answered. The lonely ring of the telephone in Dr. Mitón's (to go by the general state of the house) old-fashioned and dusty chambers could not reach its master's ear.

In principle, time should not lie heavy on one's hands in a city like Granada. How many hours can one spend in the Alhambra, or in the gardens of the Generalife, and still discover a new fountain or a new courtyard? But I just could not pass the time doing that. It was less than a year since I had seen it all with Stephanie, and it was only a fortnight since we had buried her.

So I visited the 'National Museum of Spanish–Mussulman Art' and the 'Museum of Fine Arts'. We had not had time to visit either on the previous trip, so that I need not be afraid they would arouse painful memories. On the Sunday I hired a small car and drove out to the wild and stony Sierra del Àquila, going up to the pass they call the 'Puerto del Suspiro del Moro' and looking for the spot where the unfortunate Mohammed Boabdil, the last Moorish king in Spain, had turned round for the last time, because from there one has a final glimpse of the Alhambra glinting in the sun before the stony road to the south rapidly drops down towards the coast. The verses from Heine's ballad about Boabdil's departure kept running through my head,

> On the pass where, looking northwards,
> All the valley of the Duero
> And the towers of Granada
> Spread out in a farewell vista,
> There the exiled king dismounted
> And looked back to see his city
> Gleaming in the evening sunlight
> As if decked in gold and purple . . .

but it was too hazy, or perhaps it wasn't quite the right place, anyway. I couldn't see a thing.

On both the evenings, though, I could think of nothing better to do than to go to the cinema. On the first evening there was a Spanish film. As the audience laughed, I assume it was a comedy. There is, of course, the possibility that it was seriously meant but unintentionally funny, but in such cases it is rare for everyone to laugh. In the Spanish film comedy I saw, everyone laughed, myself included, though with a delay of half a second. (Why are we so unwilling to admit that we don't understand something? Is lack of knowledge of a foreign language something shameful? Even when one can speak other foreign languages but not the one in question?) It was naturally annoying always to be the last one to laugh, so once I laughed first, but on that occasion the happenings on the screen were obviously not a joke. No one else laughed and everyone stared at me.

The next evening I had no need to monitor my reactions The film was dubbed into Spanish, but it was *Way Out West*. I don't keep a written record, but I estimate I have seen that film eight times – *Hamlet* only twice. Nowadays it's not so embarrassing to admit to something like that. I have colleagues who wallow in such confessions, in connection with something they call subculture. I have a suspicion that it is pure snobbery, especially since, on closer examination I have never come across a single one of them who has anything remotely approaching my knowledge of Laurel and Hardy.

How should we evaluate things like the Laurel and Hardy films? In his own day a writer like Nestroy (probably Shakespeare as well), who used the form of the popular theatre, was doubtless no more highly regarded – in comparison to his serious contemporaries – than Laurel and Hardy today. Would any cultured Elizabethan have dared to admit that he valued that playwright Shakespeare more highly than the presumably progressive and highly literary poet Edmund Spenser?

I have allowed myself to stray into the area of my own specialism. It wasn't in that cinema in Granada that these thoughts came to me, but just now, as I was writing down this account. When I was in Granada I was prey to a pointless but inevitable anxiety: would I have time on Monday morning to secure Stephanie's letter? Obsessively – as in an unpleasant dream in which one is vainly trying to catch a train that is about to depart from a gigantic, labyrinthine railway station – I kept calculating the limited time at my disposal before my flight left. During that time I had to: find the lawyer, explain the matter to him, obtain his permission and then drive out to the palace, find the caretaker, dig for the letter, drive back, return the rented car to Hertz, pay the hotel, pack my suitcase ... I allocated a minimal amount of time to each activity. According to my calculations, it ought to work out if I accepted that I would only reach the airport at a quarter to eleven, instead of half past ten as intended (they would presumably still let me on the plane, perhaps it would be late anyway) and assuming Dr. Mitón would be in his chambers at half past seven.

I still find getting up in the morning difficult, in spite of a profession which involves frequent early rising, but at least I have become accustomed to it. At precisely half past seven I was at the house in the Plaza Nueva where Dr. Mitón had his chambers, reading a brass plate which I had missed on Saturday and which said that Dr. Mitón's office hours were from nine to twelve.

Still I did not give up. The enforced ninety minutes of inactivity I passed in a ruminative walk through the town that was slowly waking up, past markets where all the brightly coloured fruits of Andalusia were piled up in appetising mounds, along streets where bold, romantic figures poured pails of water over the pavement with a great flourish, followed by pointless sweeping movements – presumably some ritual of purification – with an archaic broom, across squares where *hidalgos* in threadbare berets leaning against walls or wrought-iron bars had already assumed the posture of their working day, one foot resting against the wall behind, a cigarette hanging from the corner of their mouths, one eye on the newspaper: this walk through the city at a time when it was still cool, still private, at this early hour not yet plagued with foreigners, gave me the opportunity to go over my time-table for the morning once again. I should still be able to manage it, assuming I did not bother to sit down in the chair Dr. Mitón would presumably offer me, assuming, too, that I would be able to express my request clearly in five minutes and the lawyer would not spend much time reflecting on it. The best thing would be, I thought, if he just said yes. That way I would gain ten minutes. I hoped he would not have to telephone Madrid, put the request to the Duke personally, or anything like that. I am neither long-sighted nor short-sighted, but I am visually imprecise. Even though I had missed the brass plate on Dr. Mitón's door on the

Saturday, if I had read it properly, that is right through, this morning I would have saved myself an hour and a half of tormented calculation. The plate had one more line to it: Closed on Mondays. Furious with myself, I walked slowly back to the hotel and was at the airport shortly after ten. Without the letter.

The Easter holidays were the next opportunity I had to fly to Granada for a reasonable length of time – that is, for a full two weeks. In the meantime I had realised that I had only been deceiving myself with the calculations I had made on that Monday morning. Although this time I had prepared for the visit in advance by corresponding with Dr. Mitón about my request (I had to assemble a number of documents, papers of my great-aunt's, a certificate of probate for my mother's estate, etc), although Dr. Mitón was most charming and even passed on greetings from the old Duke himself, assuring me that he well remembered my great-aunt Helen, and although as a precaution I had photocopied all the documents and had them translated into Spanish, the fourteen days at my disposal – they did, of course, include those days of Holy Week and Easter when no work is done at all – were only just enough for me to achieve my goal. The most difficult part of all was to obtain the permission of the Archaeological Institute. Without Dr. Mitón's assistance I would not have not have got anywhere with them, though I am not sure whether without Dr. Mitón's good offices I would have been confronted with this difficulty at all.

'What do you mean, the Archaeological Institute?' I asked.

'The Archaeological Institute', said Dr. Mitón, 'is the body responsible whenever anything is dug up anywhere.'

'Even electric cables?' I asked.

'It could well be', said Dr. Mitón. 'However, with your aunt's diary we are dealing with a relic from the past, so to speak, and in that case digging for it is a kind of archaeology.'

The simplest approach, I later realised, especially since Stephanie's letter was not three feet but less that eighteen inches below ground, would have been simply to climb into the park in the evening or early morning by way of one of the many crumbling or broken-down portions of the surrounding wall. No one, and certainly not the Archaeological Institute, would have noticed a thing. It would only have taken fifteen minutes.

On the Friday after Easter I drove out with Dr. Mitón. He was carrying an elegant brief-case, I my spade. In the park a gentleman from the Archaeological Institute was waiting for us. It is not something I would normally have the gall to do, especially as he represented a quasi-governmental body, but seeing him standing there, every inch the official archaeologist, I could not resist offering him first go with the spade, a kind of archaeological *droit de seigneur*. He took it seriously, as a compliment, but thanked me and declined the offer.

I had only been digging for a couple of minutes when I felt the spade strike something hard. I cleared away the soil around it. It was a wooden casket, Stephanie's remarkable legacy.

Dr. Mitón, the Archaeological Institute and I had come to an agreement: in compliance with the legal requirements, the find would become the property the Spanish state. I had signed a splendid document, that even had a seal attached, in which I renounced all claim to ownership. In return I had been given permission to photograph anything we might find.

I took a picture of the casket *in situ*, and the diary – that is Stephanie's long letter, a thick notebook bound in oilcloth – was photocopied at the Archaeological Institute. Then both the casket and the letter disappeared into the archives – for good, as was perfectly obvious. I was quite happy with that. The only thing that mattered, namely what Stephanie had to say to me, I had in my possession in the form of clean, shiny photocopies, with their faint vinegary smell, in a large envelope bearing the ostentatious monogram and coat of arms of the Archaeological Institute. In the interests of justice, I feel I must also record that I was not asked to pay a single peseta, neither for Dr. Mitón's kind assistance, nor for the services of the Archaeological Institute. Initially I had been told that I would have to bear the charge of the photocopying, which would have been perfectly reasonable, but when I went with Dr. Mitón to say farewell to the Director, he had said, No, no, the Institute would consider it an honour . . .

# STEPHANIE'S 'LETTER'

*From the very beginning I have regarded my account as a mere foreword to my sister's 'letter'. I give it here in the form in which I found it. It was written in a notebook that was slightly larger than our school exercise books. It is bound in black oilcloth; the paper is unlined and stitched with coarse thread.*

*I do not know whether Stephanie would have wanted me to write all this down, never mind approved of it. As you know, I hesitated for a long time before doing so. I am an old man, and I do not wish my knowledge of these events to be buried with me. I somehow feel it would be cruel if the knowledge of them at least did not survive. Anything that sinks without trace into the depths of time becomes meaningless, and I do not want Stephanie's suffering to have been without meaning.*

Dear brother,

I do not know whether I will ever be able to return. You will be worried about me; Ferdi will worry, too. You will know where I am, and that is a comfort to me. Ferdi will think I've left him. It's terrible, I'm living a new life and yet I've stayed the same person I was before. People here think that I – that is, the Duchess – have gone out of my mind. It was the 17th here as well; today's the 24th, so a week has passed. It wasn't right to come here, but it wouldn't have been right to stay there, either. There are situations in which everything you do is wrong.

Today is the 24th September. I am living in an age which ought to be foreign to me, but isn't. Was it all predetermined? That it was to happen to *me*? Is the reason I don't find the society here foreign that it was destined for me? (But why me, of all people?) Or do human beings not vary that much with time and place? We often make the mistake of assuming that people who lived in earlier times must have been more stupid that we are. They're no more stupid and no more intelligent. The only advantage we – I'm still saying 'we' – have over people of an earlier age is that we know, or, to be more precise, have the opportunity of knowing a little more of history. But who ever takes the trouble to make use of that tiny advantage?

It's not so very different here, and yet it's terrible. Often I think no one can ever have been as alone as I am. You can't properly apprehend it, not even when, like me, you're right in the middle of it; and a good job, too, otherwise I would really become what they think I – the Duchess – am, namely mad. They treat me well. Will I ever get back? There is *one* way, and one alone. When I've written everything down I'll cut the pages out of this notebook and bury the letter in the garden, in a spot where no changes will take place. At least that's one thing it's easy for me to know. The avenue of trees on the left by the gate is just the same now as when we were both here. Of course, I ought to put that the other way round: at the moment the avenue is just the same as it will be when we will both be here in two hundred years time. I needn't worry about burying the letter, but how can I tell you there is a letter there for you? The trees in the avenue are old already, only the gate is new, it was made last year.

Do you realise that you are two hundred years away? Two hundred years is an unimaginable ocean of time.

I'd better stop writing silly things like that and concentrate on telling you what has happened.

It was the 17th here as well, the 17th September, but it's still warm here, I could feel it the moment I woke up. September here is still summer. Until now – today is the 24th, have I told you that already? – I have managed to conceal the murder. *I* killed the Duke. I cut his throat. Then I got up, the bed was full of blood. I – the Duchess, that is, but for simplicity's sake I'll say 'I' from now on – I let no one into the room. That's not as easy as it sounds. No one appears to have noticed the Duke's absence. In spite of that I have to sit outside the bedroom like a dragon to make sure no one goes in. I have a bevy of maids and other servants. I say nothing so that they won't notice I can't speak Spanish properly.

The whole affair can only be a dream. But in that case I would be doubly alone. What am I saying, doubly? I would be unutterably alone, alone among shadows. ('Mid monsters, the only sentient soul' – Goethe?*) But I do know that *he* is alive. Can that be the only other sentient soul? Does *he* come from another century as well? I don't know who he is, I just know that he exists. I know it with someone else's knowledge that is within me. I know it in the same way I know that I killed the Duke. I have someone else's hatred and someone else's love inside me.

What should I do? Will *he* come? What is he called? I will recognise him. Of course I'll recognise him, whatever he calls himself.

I won't forget you at home, not you, nor Ferdi. I worry about the two of you, more, perhaps, than than you worry about me. I'm somewhat calmer today, my dear. Who knows whether these lines will ever reach you, but if they do, then I don't want you to be confronted with the bewildering emotional outpourings of a female who is perhaps genuinely insane; I want what I write to shed light on a mysterious affair, which you might one day be able to clear up, even if I don't manage to return.

It was the ring. I assume you suspect that already. If only I'd hit on it sooner. The ring drew me here, but not the ring alone. It is as if there were bonds that cannot be severed tying me to this dreadful world here. The name of this place here and of the place where I used to live – and where I will perhaps one day again live in peace – are almost the same; the surnames begin with the same initial, even if I do have to grant the enormous difference in rank. The Duchess is (was) called Estefanía, as I am. And Ferdinand is the name of the man I am married to, both here and there. It frightens me. Did there have to be that parallel as well? And last but not

---

* Stephanie was quite right to be unsure about the quotation. In fact it is from Schiller's ballad 'The Diver'. I have to admit that I had to look it up first. I would also like to point out the remarkable anachronism: Schiller's ballad was written in 1797, Stephanie's letter in 1761 and 1762.

least, it was our great-aunt who forged the first living links. What is the point of it all? Is there any purpose behind it? I don't know.

After Easter, after we returned home from here, I didn't tell you much. I may even have been unfriendly and ungrateful towards you. I can only ask you to forgive me. But you probably noticed anyway. I had discovered the power of the ring. Now you might think that would make it easy to switch off the 'dreams', but I was not only afraid of them, I was addicted to them as well. Every evening when I was sensible and took the ring off before going to sleep I knew that sooner or later there would come an evening when I would keep it on. The more I was away, creeping round this house here, the weaker my ability to resist the terrible fascination grew.

When I made another 'excursion' here on the night of 16th September, I decided I would take the ring off before I was overcome with the leaden weariness which always seemed to be a kind of signal that I was about to return. It wasn't easy. Are my fingers fatter here, or was the ring trying to tell me not to do it? I had to. I tugged at the ring and it yielded. At the moment it's in a tiny drawer in a small table in the bedroom here. It's a secret compartment, but I found it right away: you twist a little wooden peg in the large drawer and the small drawer inside it is released. There are some of the Duchess' jewels in the compartment, including a diadem she's wearing on a picture hanging in one of the state rooms. We went through the room that time with the old custodian, it had scarlet wallpaper. The picture wasn't there then; we would certainly have noticed it if it had been, as it's a portrait of me.

After I had hidden the ring, I threw the counterpane over the corpse so that there was no blood visible and yanked at an embroidered blue-silk bellpull beside my bed. Immediately a sleepy-eyed maidservant appeared and asked what I wanted. I said nothing, I just went out into the little cubicle between the bedroom and the large room with the mosaic floor. The servant dressed me. The dress of the second half of the eighteenth century is well known, but to know it in all its incredible uncomfortableness, you would have to wear it as I do, not as a disguise or fancy dress, but for everyday use. I was laced up so tight I could hardly breathe, though in the meantime I have got used to that. What I haven't yet got used to is the fact that — excuse me for mentioning such intimate details — they dressed me up in all kinds of underwear, shifts and petticoats and stockings, but nothing in the least resembling panties or even a pair of knickers. I don't know why, but the most unaccustomed aspect of it is to feel myself so 'free' under my clothes around precisely those parts of my body. Is that the fundamental difference between women now and your women? I must admit that sometimes it has a slightly aphrodisiac effect when I'm walking in my orange grove and a gentle, late-summer Andalusian breeze manages to play upon places under my skirts that are never played on like that in your century. I admit I have to suppress impure thoughts, but I can manage that without difficulty — I just have to think of the dead man in the bedroom.

I have a whole crowd of maidservants; one is even a Moor, called Encarnación. Two of the other maids I also already know by name: an old one who evidently has authority to order the others around is called Anna, and there is a young one, on the ugly side but — or so it seems to me — very attached to me and trustworthy; she is called Josefa.

Today is the 25th September. This morning Anna told me there was something or other happening the day after tomorrow. I didn't understand exactly what it was. It seems we'll have to go to mass. I have the confidence to say something now, the occasional short sentence. There is no reaction from the maids. Of course, I have no idea what they say behind my back. I wonder if they have noticed anything? Fortunately there seem to be very few people in the palace, and no relatives at all, which is the important thing. A chaplain came to see me yesterday. I kissed his hand (that was probably overdoing it, I suppose you only do that with bishops) and sent him away again. I have the feeling I'll have to be on my guard with him.

It is quite good that they think I'm mentally deranged. That will explain a lot. But of course I mustn't appear too deranged.

I asked Josefa what the Chaplain's name was. She stared at me, wide-eyed, and said, 'Don Gonzalo'. I made a gesture as if to say, 'How could I forget!' Not a very convincing one though, I think.

I told Anna – I worked out the sentence very carefully beforehand – that the Duke had gone hunting. Does that sound plausible? Dukes certainly ride out hunting, true, but all of them? And it is a week since he 'rode out to hunt'. The smell in the bedroom is already growing unbearable. I've locked the door. If only I had a small German-Spanish dictionary!

26th September

I have to conceal things at the same time as I am trying to find things out. I must conceal the murder and I must find out what kind of life this Stephanie, whose part I am playing (or who I really am?), led. One false step could spell disaster. If only my Spanish were better! I feel like a blind person trying to find his way through a strange town on his own and having to make sure, into the bargain, that no one sees him.

The food is awful. I would never have believed that they could take such little care over hygiene in such an aristocratic household. As well as that, everything has too much salt and over half the meat dishes are made from offal, and not just liver and kidneys, either. There are things among them that I have never seen, and, as you know, I'm not a bad cook. And the animals they eat! Recently they served up roast pine-marten. I think their motto is, 'If it moves, eat it'! If I weren't so taken up with concealing my murder, I would institute meat inspection.

Now and then I play cards with Anna. Fortunately for me the Duchess' favourite game was a kind of rummy for two players. What else can I do all day when I have to keep the bedroom door under surveillance all the time. For the last few days I've been sleeping out here in the drawing-room with the flower-pattern floor. There's a sofa here. The smell is unbearable.

Today Don Gonzalo, the Chaplain, was back again. I didn't kiss his hand this time. He sat down in the salon, obviously expecting a long talk. Do you think he has no duties outside the palace? In that case, of course, he wouldn't have much to do.

Don Gonzalo wanted to know whether the Duke would be back for the ceremony tomorrow? I told him I didn't know.

I told him I had decided to study the genealogy of my family a little and he should bring me a detailed family tree. (I said *tabla genealogica*, I hope that's more or less right.)

After he had drunk a cup of chocolate and I had sat facing him in total silence for a quarter of an hour, he left.

29th September

Dear brother,

I have just read through what I wrote on the first few pages of this notebook. I have the feeling it's something of a jumble. I should have related things in the order they happened. I'll try to do that for the last few days.

I am restricted to my apartments in the palace here which consist of the bedroom you know about, the drawing-room with the floral mosaic, and the small dressing-room between the two. The dead Duke is in the bedroom, still lying there, covered over with the counterpane as I left him the morning of the day I came here. I should say I *was* restricted to them, now I have more freedom of movement. To anticipate a little: the corpse has gone. There are all sorts of doors in the bedroom, but fortunately there were keys in all the locks so that I could lock them. Even the door from the bedroom out onto the terrace with the stone steps I locked during the day; I only used to open it at night. In spite of that it soon reached the point where I could only go into the room by holding my breath. To make sure nobody – they're all inquisitive, especially the old one, Anna – went into the bedroom, I had to spend the whole day sitting on guard in the drawing-room. The day before yesterday, no, the day before the day before yesterday, the 26th, that is, the smell had already reached the drawing-room.

On the night of the 26th I locked all the doors leading into the drawing-room, took a deep breath and then made my way through the bedroom, out onto the terrace and down into he garden. There was complete silence, and I made every effort to ensure no one saw me. I believe I succeeded in this and no one did see me. I remembered on our previous ('previous'? – I ought really to say 'future') visit seeing a summer-house, a kind of small pavilion or something like that, at the bottom of the garden. And when I checked, the pavilion was still there (or 'already'; it could have been built a hundred years from now); and it was open. Inside it's full of cages in which someone (the Duke?) keeps birds. The birds didn't wake up, at least they didn't make any noise. A few cooed in their sleep. It was perhaps one hour after midnight. The fact that there were birds in the summerhouse, a surprise factor in my calculations, both favoured my plan and signalled a risk. The birds stank to high heaven, more even, that I realised immediately, than the Duke's corpse. But someone will have to feed the birds, clean out their cages and so on. That is, someone will visit the pavilion regularly and often. In spite of that, I decided to take the body of the Duke there. The summerhouse didn't seem to be inhabited, in the sense that someone lived there.

I went back to the bedroom – yes, I did it all myself, with my own hands, with these hands you know so well. The most horrible of all the horrors of those two hours came as I was dragging the Duke down the flight of stone steps and the corpse – I had tied it up it in the sheet, which, fortunately, was both large and strong – bumped against each step. But the fear that someone might see me was even stronger than the horror of it, otherwise I probably wouldn't have been able to do it at all. I was genuinely relieved when I at least had the corpse down in the garden in the shadow of the trees. Trees cast shadows by night as well, even blacker ones than by day.

I dragged the corpse all the way to the little pavilion. I couldn't carry it, it was too heavy. It wasn't bleeding any more. That was another cause for relief. I had been afraid I would have had traces of blood to clear up all the way from the palace to the summerhouse.

The pavilion has three rooms: the large room with the birdcages and lots of windows giving onto the park, a room on the left by the entrance, which is empty, and a room at the back. This last room contains junk. There's also a cupboard in it, a large cupboard. As there's another cupboard exactly the same in the main room at the front, I assume this one was taken out of the front room and brought in here because they needed the space it occupied for birdcages. So the cupboard would probably be unused. It was also pretty dusty. The key was in the lock.

I crammed the Duke into the cupboard, locked him in and took the key with me. At first I was going to lock the door to the rear chamber as well (the key to that was in the lock, too) but then I left it. Someone might notice. Locked doors arouse more curiosity than open ones.

I haven't been back since then, but it's obvious that the cupboard can only be a temporary resting place for the Duke. I've thought up all sorts of ideas, throwing him into the river, for example, or having him carried down into the family vault and put into someone else's coffin. But for that I'd have to take someone into my confidence. Josefa?

My immediate reaction was one of relief, no, it was like being brought back to life now that the corpse was at least out of the bedroom. Naturally there was still a smell. Also I had to get rid of all the bloodstained bedclothes. I took those to the summerhouse as well, but then couldn't bring myself to open up the cupboard, so I stuffed them underneath. I'll burn them when – and if – the opportunity presents itself. There is a fireplace there.

One fortunate aspect is that the mattresses are only slightly smudged with blood. I swapped them over but, God knows, it's not going to be easy since I'll have to sleep on them to avoid attracting attention. I mean, what I did was to put the mattress from the Duke's side of the bed on mine, and vice versa. I also turned them over, bloody side down. I intend to put Josefa in charge of the bedroom and I'll tell her it was me; perhaps the thought will occur to her anyway, women bleed occasionally, and here there are no medicines for it yet. Then I remade the Duke's bed. In the little cubicle on the other side of the bedroom I found a huge linen cupboard full of sheets and blankets. I don't think anyone will notice that one set is missing. After all that, I was astonished the whole thing didn't take more than two hours – and that included smoothing out the gravel, where I had dragged the corpse along over it, with a broom I found behind the cages in the pavilion. For the rest of the night I left all the doors and windows open. Although there was only a gentle night breeze, there was quite a draught. I can't say whether the stench has gone completely, since it will be weeks before I can get it out of my own system, but I think I can risk letting Josefa into the bedroom tomorrow.

I'll have to break off now, the Chaplain has just been announced. Perhaps he's bringing my family tree. At the very least he'll want his cup of chocolate.

30th September

It's raining. Josefa said that autumn's coming and immediately had the fire lit. It still doesn't make the room warm. This palace is a summer residence. I get on very well with Josefa. Our conversations improve my fluency; I read a lot, too, for the practice, not out of interest, since all the books lying around the rooms here are devotional literature. Duchess Estefanía must have been extremely devout, or at least put on a pious air. I have not come across any other books. I haven't yet managed to find the Duke's library. Perhaps the boorish oaf didn't have one.

One thing that I often find disconcerting is Josefa's reaction, or rather, her complete lack of reaction when, despite all my care, I make mistakes in my Spanish. If – and this seems obviously to be the case – I look like the Duchess, then I probably have the same voice as hers. But the Duchess will not have made mistakes in her mother tongue. Moreover it's very unlikely that I have precisely the same gestures, habits and so on as she did. Quite apart from the mistakes in my Spanish, it is out of the question that none of those who were close to the Duchess will have noticed anything. I keep on emphasising that I am ill, I pretend to be absentminded and a little mad, but is that enough? There are some circumstances here that are clearly in my favour. First of all, for the people here I *am* the Duchess. However bizarre my behaviour, no one could possibly suspect that I might not be the real Duchess, whatever strange things I do. They may have all sorts of explanations for the way I behave, but it's impossible they should hit on the true one. Secondly, the Duchess seems to have been attended primarily by the old servant, Anna. I prefer Josefa, who clearly was not as close to the Duchess before, I can tell that by the things she doesn't know, the things she has to go and ask about. Josefa has less precise means of comparison.

Anna withdrew in pique when she noticed that 'now' I prefer Josefa. She sent me a message via the Chaplain telling me she was deeply hurt that she had fallen into disfavour after she had served me, my mother, and even my grandmother for over fifty years. I replied by the same route to the effect that it had nothing to do with disfavour, but that I wanted to make things easier for her in her old age. I accompanied my reply with a few gold coins. In a writing desk in the drawing-room there is a casket containing money; the key is in the secret drawer, along with the jewelry, so I assume the money belongs to 'me'. The ridiculous thing about it is that I have no idea what the money is worth. Was it too much? Or too little? Was it right to send it at all? The Chaplain's reaction suggested it was probably rather a lot of money; he just stared at it, horrified, or at least that was my impression, and was unwilling to take it from me. I hope he will actually give it to her. I can't help it, but I think he's a rogue.

So far no one has asked after the Duke. Now, after almost two weeks, I can hardly imagine anyone still believes the story that he has ridden out to hunt. But I harbour a suspicion which reassures me somewhat: people will assume that it was the Duke who lied to me about going hunting. I assume he often used to 'go out hunting'. And I can well imagine *what* he was hunting. When I've had more practise in my Spanish and can risk such complicated sentences, I'll sound out Josefa. Simply speaking the language I no longer find that difficult; I often surprise myself how some things, even quite difficult ones, just seem to trip off my tongue. But what I do find difficult is to speak as quickly as people here and to shout all the time as they do. They always all talk at once, I live in a constant hubbub of confused voices. Of course, there are advantages in that for me. At the mass last Saturday, for example, I met my aristocratic relatives, all those dukes and duchesses, counts and countesses. As far as I could tell from the scraps of conversation I managed to understand, it was a mass in memory of the Queen, who died a year ago, a requiem on the anniversary of her death. To my astonishment, all the great lords and ladies were silent during the mass, or at least they only whispered; but before and afterwards Pandemonium reigned. They jabber on, this way and that way and every other way, and all at top speed. I don't think anyone noticed that I didn't say a word.

I was driven to Granada in a beautiful carriage. It took three hours for a journey we did in the car in twenty minutes. (Here and now, no one counts time in minutes. That's something else I had to get used to. The smallest unit of time they recognise is a quarter of an hour. The minute seems to be regarded more as a piece of scientific tomfoolery of no practical value for real life.) Anna came with us – that was before I sent her the money via the Chaplain – but I also took Josefa. There was Don Gonzalo too, of course, and a few lackeys. There is a sort of head lackey called Alejandro who seems to be a nephew or some other close relative of Anna's.

After the mass there was a kind of reception in a palace.

There was no great danger, so I just went along. I think the clerical gentleman who shook us all by the hand must be the Bishop of Granada. (Or is he an archbishop? Or even a cardinal? I wish I was as well-up in these matters as you are.) There was a lot of talk about whether the King will marry again or not, and if he does, then whom. It would be a blessing if at least I had a newspaper, but newspapers obviously haven't been invented yet, not in Spain anyway. We – Spain that is – seem to be at war with England. After I heard that, I went over what we learnt at school, and if I remember correctly, it ought to be the Seven Years War. Were Spain and England at war with each other then, or was that a separate war? Until now I had assumed it was Prussia against Austria, but Portugal also seems to be involved in it, and on England's side.\*

After that the tongues got down to pulling the eligible daughters of various royal houses to pieces. There is a French princess, Adelaide, I think, who is considered too old. (Just imagine, too old at 29!) One of the Austrian archduchesses is called Marie Christine and, according to my Chaplain, who's always holding forth, (you see, I'm already saying 'my Chaplain', I must be beginning to feel I belong) she's of the right age, nineteen, but she's considered to be her mother's – the Empress' – favourite daughter, and she wouldn't marry her off to someone so far away. Would that be the Empress Maria Theresa? I suppose it must – the Seven Years War, I remember now; here they think her a venomous old shrew. There was talk of a Bavarian princess too, Antonia she's called, and of one by the name of Maria Ernestina d'Este from Modena.

---

\* Since my sister here touches on an area in which I have a professional interest, I cannot refrain from appending a footnote. It is the case that in 1761 Spain, following the so-called 'Bourbon Family Compact' of 17th August 1761, was at war on the side of the French against England and Portugal. This war, which was indeed a kind of side-issue of the Seven Years War, is more or less unknown, and justly so since it produced hardly any serious military engagements, had no political consequences and petered out in 1762.

But there was something much more important: I've seen *him*.

Just as I knew straight away where the little secret compartment in the drawer was, so I also know all the little secret compartments in the soul of that poor woman I now have to be. And I also know what's in those secret compartments. It's very confusing. You can't write it down, and even if you could, no one would understand it unless they could understand it without seeing it written down.

I didn't talk to *him*, but he's different from the others. He's taller, and he isn't as fat as most of the men. He wears a military uniform and a cloak with a cross embroidered on it. Whilst he was talking to the Bishop he was looking across at me. I didn't dare ask who he is. All I know is that I've known him for a long time.

Nobody, as far as I could tell, noticed the Duke's absence. And another thing: after a short time there was an awful smell in the room. No one opened a window, perhaps that's not usual. I can't help it, but I have the feeling none of them ever wash. After a quarter of an hour the room smelt like a canteen hut on a building site in the middle of winter. We had lunch in a small inn about half way between Granada and here. I didn't need to give orders for it, clearly that's what always happens.

We stepped down from the carriage. The innkeeper greeted us and was greatly honoured, although we didn't eat anything from his kitchen. We had brought everything with us, in a leather trunk: crockery and cutlery, all silver, a vanity-case; there were baskets full of cold roast meat, chicken, cakes and all sorts of things. Anna had prepared everything. I do not deny that she is a jewel. All we had from the innkeeper was the wine.

We just can't imagine what it's like any more, even I keep having to remind myself who I am. Without further ado, the innkeeper just threw all his customers out of all his rooms (he has three). I was going to tell Anna that at least they could stay in the two other rooms, but the innkeeper's adamant insistence was such a matter of course, as was the reaction of the people, who didn't complain at all, they thought it quite right and proper. Not only that, they seemed to be happy to be thrown out of the inn for my sake. The innkeeper's wife brought her children, and they kissed my hand. Word that I had stopped there must have got round, for half an hour later a few young girls arrived and kissed my hand, followed by several old women. Shortly before we left, a particularly filthy old woman came. She stank like a cesspit. She had brought her grown-up son, a cretin. He looked like a bloated six-year-old and was so knock-kneed he could hardly walk. His mother had to half carry him. Anna interpreted for me: I was to bless the son. (The old woman spoke in a dialect of which I could not understand a word, her son just babbled.) I objected that that was a task for Don Gonzalo. Immediately the old woman started to cry and her son joined in, howling till the snot was pouring from his nose. Upon my soul, I've never seen anything like it. For people like us, like you and me, that is, it's a terrible irritation if a single fly lands on our skin, it tickles, and we brush it off. The unfortunate young man had dozens of flies pecking at the snot on his upper lip and he didn't seem to feel a thing.

So in God's name I blessed him as well as I could. You cannot imagine the depths of squalor the poor live in at this time. I'm not surprised that history is going to take the turn which I already know about, though to my shame I must admit my knowledge is pretty sketchy. Those people who were shooed out of the inn just because some rich duchess wanted to have her picknick there – there only needs to be *one* among them whose wits are slightly less dull, and he must ask himself, 'Why?' That can only lead to revolution. But perhaps I'm just getting hold of the wrong end of the stick and that's not the way it is at all.

I instructed Anna to give the poor old woman a gold coin. Anna gave her a silver coin. If we had given her a gold coin, the Chaplain said, word would have gone round like lightning and tomorrow the palace would have been surrounded by beggars from all over Granada, the day after tomorrow those from Jaén, Guadix and Antequera would be there, and by next week at the latest all the beggars from the whole of Andalusia would be encamped round the palace, whilst the beggars from the united kingdoms of Castile and Aragon would be on their way. Then each would get one silver coin, I said. Then they'll stay, said Anna. Then we'll cook soup for them, I said, there's plenty for everyone. But beggars don't only beg, said the Chaplain, beggars also steal, at least there's always a few among them who will make off with something should the opportunity arise, it's only natural. God forbid that too many beggars should gather in our district. They're like locusts. Just think of your peasants, their fields would be stripped bare, not even the cabbage stalks would be safe. No child would be safe, either, not to mention the chickens and sheep. There would be mayhem. Do you want to make your people unhappy? ('Your people' – that's the peasants of the surrounding area, clearly they 'belong' to me.) Do you want to make beggars of your people? Give the old woman this silver coin, as an act of charity it is both generous and appropriate.

I left it at that. Anna gave the old woman the silver coin. It would be a lie if I said I was happy with it. The old woman kissed my hand and started singing. ('She always sings', said Anna, 'that's her way of saying thank you.')The young cripple joined in at first, but then fell silent, at which the old woman, without interrupting her singing, gave him a kick. The lad immediately gave a howl, though I don't know whether that was crying or singing. The old woman's singing was getting more and more out of tune, but she kept on going until Anna jerked her head vigorously. Immediately the old woman stopped singing, kissed my hand again and sobbed something which, of course, I could not understand. Her imbecile son received another kick, at which he also kissed, or rather licked my hand. It wasn't very hygienic. Then they left. If I really did have the power to bless, I would have blessed the old woman and her son.

But that's not the end of the story.

Through the window I could see that the old woman had deposited some things, presumably her baggage, outside: a large, indescribably dirty sack and a remarkably awkward object which somewhat resembled a folded deck-chair. The old woman was trying to load the sack onto her son's back, but without success, he was too clumsy, the sack kept falling down. I could see that the idiot boy was not unwilling, he just couldn't manage it. Eventually the mother took up the sack herself.

At that, I gave an order. There were three lackeys with us, not counting Alejandro, the head lackey; while we were driving, one sat on the box with Alejandro and the coachman, the other two at the back. At that moment they were stuffing themselves in the kitchen. I gave the order for one of these young louts to help the old woman carry her things.

Anna passed on the order, but very unwillingly. Naturally the lackeys then argued among themselves as to who should undertake this unpleasant task. Then one of them came in with a sullen look on his face and asked again what he was supposed to do. The Chaplain went out with him, then he came back in: where should the lackey help the old woman carry her things *to*? Wherever she's going, I said. She won't live in a fine mansion, but she must have somewhere to live. No, said the Chaplain, she doesn't live anywhere, does the lackey have to go with the old woman for ever? Stupid question, but what was I to do now? I decreed that the lackey was to accompany her to the next village. He was back very quickly. I guess the whole thing must have been more trouble than it was worth for the old woman.

Then something else happened in the bodega, or rather it happened beforehand. A man on horseback turned up, and not, it seemed to me, by chance. The man, who affected to be younger than he quite obviously was, was addressed by the Chaplain and Anna as 'Chevalier', though he was Italian. Don Gonzalo and Anna, usually as thick as thieves, seem to be at variance over the Chevalier. Anna eyed him suspiciously, as if she were afraid he would steal one of the silver spoons, while he was on intimate terms with the Chaplain. He spoke to me as if he had known me for a long time, respectfully, but as between people who are of more or less the same class. He's probably one of the friends of the late Duke. I know what kind of friends they would be.

For the rest of the journey home the Chevalier trotted along beside the carriage then, later on, he rode on ahead. One of the extra horses was saddled for the Chaplain, who went with him. Clearly the Chevalier must have spent that night here in the palace. Anna gave me a hint when she asked for my instructions about the guest and dinner. I told her very firmly that I intended to dine alone.

Yesterday – no, it's past midnight already, the day before yesterday, on Monday, the Chevalier waited upon me and took his leave. I was very curt with him. That means he spent two days in the house, during which time the Chaplain didn't put in an appearance in my rooms at all. I asked Josefa. She said the Chevalier and the Chaplain had ridden out to hunt.

I'll go to the summerhouse this very night and see if I can't get rid of the blood-stained bedlinen. I feel even more afraid of that than of last week's much more gruesome task.

Goodnight, brother. Allow me one silly remark. Leaving aside the question of whether you will ever read this letter, where are you, now that I am here? Do you exist? What nights are they that lie between us, perhaps will always lie between us?

2nd October

Dear brother, this is it; things are getting serious. Who knows whether you will ever read this letter. Probably you'll never see it, but I'm still writing it, in spite of that. When I write in this notebook, I have the feeling I'm talking to you, and that's my only refuge, my only comfort on this far-off, ice-cold shore of time on which I have been cast up. Today is the anniversary of father's death. Dear father! He hasn't even been born yet, here, now, where I am compelled to live. A retrospective anniversary, if you like. He will die in one hundred and ninety-one years from today, if the calendar for 1761 I found among the Duchess' things is this year's. It's a very pious calendar. Every day has at least four Saints or

Blesseds; today it's the turn of Dietburga, Leodegar, Custodius, Hildebold and Berga. I can't really ask Josefa what year it is, and it's not written anywhere like the names of towns at railway stations. But I guess it will be this year's calendar. There are some short hand-written entries – by the Duchess, I assume – on dates that are presumably important. Tomorrow, for example, is the birthday of the Dauphine. That will be the Crown Princess of France, I suppose. I don't know whether it's celebrated here, perhaps it is since we – 'we' Spaniards – are allied with France, if I've understood the situation correctly.

But that's not what I was going to tell you about. I wanted to tell you that it seems as if the moment has arrived. It was Josefa who told me. I can't remember, did I tell you about the disagreeable horseman who joined us during our stop at the inn between Granada and here? I can't look back to check just now, as I want to get all this written down; who knows what else I'll have to do during this night. I don't want to look back, either, I don't like reading things I've written myself, even at school I never read my essays over before handing them in – unlike you, I know.

Josefa is bringing the light. It's not so simple, here and now, you can't just go to a switch and 'turn on the light'. If you need it to be brighter, the light is brought into the room. It does have the advantage that it never suddenly becomes light. That never happens, except when there's lightning. That's something you in the twentieth century can't imagine, that it never becomes light *all of a sudden*. When Josefa brings the light as it's getting dark, around six o'clock, then what I see is – let's say I'm sitting at my embroidery (I have indeed taken up embroidery; what won't a body do out of boredom! I'm working on an embroidery the Duchess seems to have begun, a huge, colourful floral pattern, a round tablecloth, I suspect), anyway, there I am, sewing, as I was yesterday, for example – today I'm writing this letter, of course – and as the twilight deepens I move closer and closer to the window until even there it's too dark, and I call for the light or, as happens most often, my Josefa has already thought of it herself and brings the light before I can ask, then at first I only see a shimmer out in the hall, coming nearer and flickering because it's a candelabra that's being carried and because there's almost always a draught in a palace like this, then the doorway is filled with golden, living light – it ought to be sad for you not to be able to know these things; excuse me for saying so, but the water closet cannot fully compensate for it – the doorway is filled with golden, flickering light; at first none of it comes into the room, it's as if the doorway were a barrier to the light, an impenetrable film of air; the candlelight makes the film curve inwards, into the room, and only when Josefa comes through the door does the film burst and the room becomes bright, but never as bright as in your century, never illuminating every last nook and cranny. That's how it is, light never takes you by surprise, and I can understand, now, why the shepherds in the fields outside Bethlehem were sore afraid: it was because it had become light all of a sudden.

Josefa was here with the light just now. I told her to leave me alone for a few moments until I've finished writing, then she's to come back and we'll discuss what we're to do.

I've written so much already. If instead of that I'd looked back at what I wrote the day before yesterday, I would know whether I have already mentioned the disagreeable man. He calls himself Chevalier de Florimonte and is one of those men who imagine they are very handsome. He is Italian, they say, and a friend of the Duke's. I can very well imagine that he is. There is no doubt that the meeting at the inn was not a coincidence. The Chaplain went outside several times, presumably to see if the Chevalier was coming. He must have been delayed, for when the Chaplain noticed that I was thinking of setting off, he became restless and began darting to and fro like a fly in a glass.

The Chevalier is one of those men who, in the presence of a woman, behave as if they had eyes for her alone. One of the type of men who say of themselves that they were made for women; the kind of man who sits at our feet. I knew a man like that once – I kept him well away from you and the family, it was ages before Ferdi, and it didn't last long, either – and he always used to say, 'When I look into your eyes, I forget everything else.' Perhaps some women like that; I don't. Of course, to get back to the Chevalier de Florimonte, it was stupid of me to do the worst thing a woman can do to a man like that: I ignored him. The Chaplain brought him to my table in the inn and said, 'But your Grace,' (that's the way they address me) 'this is the Chevalier de Florimonte, surely your Grace remembers?' The Chevalier stood there beside him, putting on his roguish look, a kind of charming sidelong glance which he probably thinks is manly, but which a woman like myself would at best find sweet in a dog, if I liked dogs. But I don't like them, as you know. So I said, 'No, Chaplain, I don't remember the Chevalier, not that I can say.'

However, I have the feeling that it wasn't that that made an enemy of the vain booby; he was already my enemy, the Duchess' enemy, I mean.

When we drove on then, he rode beside my carriage for a while, somewhat nonplussed. The Chaplain was on horseback now, too, he'd had one of the extra horses saddled, and when the two gentlemen got fed up with riding along beside the carriage being ignored by me, they rode on ahead.

That all happened on the Saturday; today is Thursday, so it was nearly a week ago. The Chevalier stayed here in the palace, they told me, but I never invited him to eat with me. The Chaplain came to see me and deluged me in longwinded, snivelling reproaches; he went on and on, without getting to the point, so that for a long time I had no idea what he was after. He gave me to understand that it was outrageously impolite of me not to invite the Chevalier to table. The Duchess, it seems, treated him better, although I can't imagine she liked him. Then I had an inspiration which really got to the heart of the matter. I said I would invite him to dine with me the moment he showed me his patent of nobility. On Tuesday the Chevalier left without my seeing him again.

You might say, perhaps are saying if you are reading this letter, that it is unwise to antagonise people who have their fingers in matters that concern me. *I* say it is more important to keep such people at a distance, not to give them the opportunity of observing me.

Today Josefa made the revelation which led me to remark that things seem to be getting serious.

In the afternoon she was sorting out my underwear, storing freshly washed items in the cupboards, putting ones that needed repairing on one side and so on, a job that she normally never does herself, only supervises. She was busying herself about the bedroom, I was playing patience in the sitting-room (the room with the beautiful floral mosaic on the floor). The doors were open.

'The Chevalier's left', Josefa said.

'I know', I said.

'Tuesday morning', she said.

'I know', I said.

'Don Gonzalo left too', she said.

'I know', I said.

'Tuesday afternoon', she said.

'Josefa', I said, 'if there's something you want to tell me, come through here so we don't have to shout at each other.'

She came through to the drawing-room.

'He took *Jupiter*', she said.

'Who is Jupiter?'

'Now you're even forgetting who Jupiter is', said Josefa. 'The fast horse.'

'Oh, that Jupiter', I said, as if I'd suddenly remembered. 'So?'

'I don't know if his Grace, the Duke, would like Don Gonzalo of all people taking Jupiter.'

'He wouldn't?' I asked.

'But, your Grace! Isn't his Grace, the Duke, always saying his sanctimonious arse would ruin any horse?'

'Is he?'

'Forgive me, but yes, he is always saying that. A man who's never . . . his Grace always uses a very rude word . . . who's never, you know, a woman, can't ride a horse either. His

Grace puts it in a somewhat different way, of course, a more forthright way, if you see what I mean.'

'I would never have believed it of his Grace!'

'Jupiter is the only horse you can take and be in Granada in the evening even if you don't set off until after vespers.'

'So?'

'He went to Granada because he was meeting the Chevalier there.'

'But he didn't have to go to Granada to do that, he could have met him here, as often as he wanted. The Chevalier honoured us with his presence for three days.'

'But he's meeting Conde Almaviva.'

'Who is this Conde Almaviva?'

'But your Grace knows Conde Almaviva?'

'I must admit the name does sound vaguely familiar.'

'He's another one.'

'Another one what?'

'Like – the Chevalier . . .'

'. . . and the Duke, you were going to say.'

'Your Grace . . .', I could see that Josefa had something very serious on her mind.

'Come and sit down', I said. 'What is it?'

'Does your Grace know where his Grace, the Duke, is?'

I gathered up the cards. The patience had come out. (I only play the kind of patience that always comes out.)

'Yes', I said, 'yes, Josefa, I know where the Duke is.'

'The two of them, the Chaplain and the Chevalier, searched the whole palace, on Saturday night.'

'Ahh . . .' I was, as you can imagine, rather perturbed.

'Yes', said Josefa, 'I only heard about it today. By chance. I was in the room behind the kitchen and I heard Anna talking to Alejandro. Anna knows everything. She obviously got it from the groom who sleeps at the front over the coachhouse. He was woken by the sound of steps from the loft above his room. I don't know what precisely happened, but he seems to have crept up the ladder and seen the two of them, the Chaplain and the Chevalier, searching the loft.'

'Why would they search the loft of the coach-house of all places?'

'They didn't only search the loft of the coach-house, they searched everywhere, the whole palace.'

'Josefa . . .'

'Yes, your Grace?'

'Did they also . . . did they also search the garden?'

'Yes, the garden as well, including . . .'

'Including the summerhouse with the birds?'

Josefa nodded.

'Well', I said, 'and what did they find?'

'Does your Grace know what they might find?'

'Have a look to see there's no one listening at the door.'

Josefa went and had a look. There was no one there, not at any of the doors.

'Blood', I said. 'They might find blood.'

'Lord preserve us! Your Grace, where do you think it will end if your Grace knows things like that!?'

'Josefa, the Duke is dead.'

'Jesus and Mary have mercy on us!' said Josefa and clapped her hand to her mouth.

'Does it surprise you to hear it?'

Josefa lowered her eyes. She kissed my hand. I raised her up again.

'It doesn't surprise you. How could it be otherwise? And now, if you know, tell me what they found.'

'Bed-linen', said Josefa, 'that was soaked in blood. The Chevalier packed it up and took it with him.'

'They didn't find anything else?'

'No. Is there something else to find?'

'There was nothing else they found?'

'Anna said it must have been terrible. She had it from the groom who watched through one of the few windows which, if you'll excuse the expression, isn't covered in bird-shit. In the dark the Chevalier is afraid of everyone and everything. They pulled the bed-linen out from under the cupboard, and at that very moment it started to strike twelve. They both turned as white as the sheets they had pulled out, the groom said, and they shot out of the pavilion and back to the palace as quick as if the Devil himself were on their heels.'

'But there's still one thing I don't understand', I said. 'Before that, they'd searched the whole palace. That must take hours, and they can't have started before ten o'clock on Saturday, the Chaplain was here with me at ten o'clock . . .'

'No', said Josefa, 'that was the second night, Sunday night. On Saturday night they searched the palace. They even took Anna with them for that. The Chaplain said he was looking for an old chronicle with a family tree of his Grace's ancestors which your Grace had asked him for.'

'Aha', I said. 'And what did they get up to on Monday night?'

'They rode out to the hunting lodge at Quiebro, but they can't have made a very thorough search, since they were back before midnight. They probably hadn't got over the shock they had the previous night.'

'You can't expect to find something you're afraid of', I said.

'Now I really don't understand what your Grace is talking about', said Josefa.

'It's all right', I said. 'You can go now, but don't tell anyone anything about this.'

'Whatever is your Grace thinking of?' said Josefa.

I began writing this down as soon as Josefa had gone. That's why I can still remember every word of our conversation, more or less every single word. The odd word here or there might not be right, but that's not important. In the meantime Josefa has brought the light and I told her to wait outside in the vestibule, I'd call her. I'm going to do that now. I don't think I should tell her everything, although I do have the feeling *she* is to be trusted. But I shouldn't expect her to be an accessory to *everything*. Goodnight, brother.

Saturday, 4th October

Human beings are by nature tough. Or you might say they are driven by inertia. Whatever the situation a person gets into, however bizarre the situation might be – and I make so bold as to say, 'Who would know better than I?' – the moments in which one recognises the full extent of one's difficulties, the seriousness of one's position, if you like, are remarkably rare. There is a law of inertia by which one's lethargic spirit tries to return to its set ways. It wants to be the way it always was. Look at me here: I'm hungry, I yawn, I'm bored, I'm pleased, sometimes I feel comfortable, sometimes I feel uncomfortable and tell Josefa to close the door as there's a draught, all as if there were nothing to it. Sometimes I'm cheerful, sometimes I look out of the window, without thinking, as if I belonged. And yet . . . and yet if you think about it properly, I'm a ghost. Recently I caught myself saying to Josefa, 'One day I'm going to freeze to death on this stone floor, Josefa, I want a carpet laid over it, a red one.' I just said it, as if everything really belonged to me, as if I belonged here, as if I had the right to feel cold here and, what's more, the right to arrange things so I stop feeling cold; as if I weren't a ghost, a ghost that has a murder to conceal.

By the way, Count Almaviva arrived today, but more of that later.

Or is it all the others who are ghosts? Are all those around me, the Chaplain and his dubious friend the Chevalier de Florimonte, Anna, the Moorish chambermaid Encarnación, Count Almaviva and the man I must tell you about soon, are they all shadows? Am I the only real person? Can I sit here by the fire in the brazier, which Josefa is just bringing in, can I lean against Josefa to feel the comforting breath of another human being, if she is only a shadow? Have I fallen into some mild version of hell surrounded by incredibly high, unscalable, overhanging rocky cliffs? With two centuries of spiders' webs and mould and bones above me, so that there isn't even a crack through which I can see the sky of my own century? Sometimes I think that this letter to you is one such crack, but who knows if it will ever reach you? By the way, I'm going to put it into a casket when it's finished – when will it be finished? – and bury it for you. When we came *before*, we saw that avenue of trees from the palace gate to the main entrance. Since, in that distant future time, the avenue will still be where it is now, I know that it will remain unchanged. If I bury the casket with the letter under a particular tree, then it will be safe, or comparatively safe. Even if, should I ever return, I can only whisper a few words to you, I can tell you where you can find it.

Now all this writing has made me restless and mournful. And when I sat down to continue the letter, I was, thanks to the natural inertia of the human spirit, almost happy, or at least reasonably cheerful. Now my worries are back. I was going to describe the picture that at the beginning played a certain role in what, for a time, I thought was a dream. I mean the picture in the bedroom with the gleaming gold frame I caught a glimpse of the first time I was here. When we were here *before* (I wish there was a word for that 'before' that comes after!) you didn't go into the bedroom. The bedroom obviously hadn't been used for a long time (won't be used any more, I presumably ought to say). Out of superstition, perhaps? Because on the night of the 16th September, 1761, I slit the Duke's throat in that bed over there? The bedroom was covered in dust and spiders' webs. The furniture was still there, but not the picture. Perhaps the heirs will sell it. The title will go to a somewhat distant cousin of the late lamented Duke, I do know that from the family tree Don Gonzalo brought me. The cousin is called Fernando and naturally, at the moment, knows nothing about it. It has just occurred to me that perhaps you would like more precise details: the late lamented Fernando, the IX Duque, had no brothers or sisters at all; his father, the VIII Duque, who was called – I'll give you three guesses – Fernando, had only sisters, five of them, I think. Two got married and three went into a convent. One is still alive, one of the married ones, Isabella, Marquesa de Villahermosa. She was there at the requiem for the anniversary of the Queen's death last week. She's a jolly old lady, well over seventy, and I think I could easily come to like her ... if she weren't another of these cold shadows. You have to go back to the grandfather, who, remarkably, was called *Juan*, to find a Duque who had brothers, two of them, an older one who was the VI Duque before him (he was called – surprise, surprise! – Fernando), and a younger one, Don Francisco, who must have been a bigwig at the King's court and died not long ago. The grandson of this Don Francisco is the aforementioned Don Fernando. He lives in Madrid and, if I can believe Josefa, is very fat, has a goitre the size of a breadbag and lots of children. Apparently for a few years now he's had his eye on the inheritance, since after ten years of marriage 'I' still haven't produced an heir. 'We' are very rich, you see, and the collateral line has no money at all because, firstly, the said Don Francisco, the bigwig, failed to use his positions in the government to enrich himself and, secondly, what little he did acquire he squandered in his later years and bequeathed the rest, such as it was, not to his children and grandchildren, but to a monastery. (I had that from the Chaplain.)

I was going to describe the picture, but I'll do it another time, when I get round to it.

Count Almaviva has arrived. He seems to be on fairly familiar terms with the Chaplain too, but I don't find him quite as repulsive as the Chevalier de Florimonte. And the Chaplain doesn't take the kind of liberties with him he does with the Chevalier. As I had plenty of opportunity to observe, he used to talk to the Chevalier as to an equal, as one rogue to another. So I can't get out of asking the Count to dine with me. I've ordered a band for this evening.

Oh yes, what else did I tell Josefa yesterday evening? I told her almost everything. No, actually I didn't have to tell her anything, she had already guessed. I'm glad she did. Did it relieve my conscience? Or just remove some of the fear? Whatever it is, I've been much more cheerful since Josefa has learnt more or less everything. She's very intelligent; she's even cunning.

To put it briefly: the Duke is still in the cupboard, but the cupboard is no longer in the pavilion. It was Josefa's idea. It didn't take her long at all to think it up. She has a clear, logical mind. His Grace, the late lamented Duke, has to go, she said, that is clear. Two weak women like us can't get rid of him and anyway, we don't want to have to look in the cupboard. Who knows what his Grace'll look like by this time. So the cupboard has to be removed. Two weak women like us can't carry the cupboard, so we'll have to find some other way to do it. And we found a way to do it yesterday. Josefa got two servants to push it out of the summerhouse and load it onto a cart. She told them the Duchess (me, that is) was going to give it to a needy convent. Some other servants then drove the cart with the cupboard out to the hunting lodge at Quiebro and parked it there. Then two huntsmen, who live out there most of the year and have no contact with the servants here, unloaded the cupboard and put it in a tumbledown old stable. Josefa went out specially to supervise it. Before the removal began, Josefa herself tied ropes round the cupboard so that it wouldn't burst open.

It does mean, Josefa says, that there are a couple of people who know something of what's going on, but it wouldn't have been possible without them and anyway, some of them are so stupid they'll forget it after a couple of hours. To make things even safer, my clever Josefa had all the furniture taken out of the pavilion and actually gave one or two pieces, including a wall-cupboard, to a convent on the edge of the town. The nuns were rather surprised and had no use for it, but ended up accepting it out of politeness. On top of that, Josefa has had lots of other pieces of furniture moved around: in the palace, up to the hunting lodge, down from upstairs, to the town house, from the town house out here and so on. At this very moment some of the staff are transporting furniture from one place to another. That way, no one particular piece will attract attention, says Josefa.

I mustn't get carried away (unlike the Duke), but it is a much relieved sister that wishes you goodnight, dear brother.

Sunday afternoon, 5th Oct.

Since yesterday nothing has happened at all. I have the feeling nothing has happened for an eternity. When, like me, you've spent days, three weeks almost, sort of sleeping with a corpse — it sounds funny now, although that's not the way I feel about it – and then hidden a corpse in a cupboard where it could be discovered any minute, when every moment you're expecting it all to come out, when you think there must be something odd going on if it doesn't come out, when, after all that, a whole day goes by without anything happening, a day when there is nothing you imagine could happen, then you immediately start thinking there's been peace and quiet for an eternity and, above all, that things will stay peaceful and quiet.

Naturally that's an illusion. The Count is still here. But so far there's been nothing, apart from what fills the day of a lady of my 'station' on her country estate: boredom.

They're still trundling furniture back and forth, under Josefa's supervision, but not so much as in the two days before; just a departing rumble, so to speak. Josefa has become very strict. It's splendid to see the way she orders them around, and yet when I 'arrived' here, she was a rather quiet young girl and completely under Anna's thumb. Now she's the one cracking the whip. The way you change when you find yourself in a position of authority! (It applies to me too, as I'm sure you can imagine.)

The servants are beginning to be afraid of Josefa. Anna doesn't like that, of course. There seems to have been something of a row between the pair of them yesterday. I asked Josefa, but she just said it was nothing, nothing, your Grace, we just gave each other a piece of our minds. Anna has intimated rather indignantly that she was surprised we were not gradually getting down to preparing for our return to the town house, as happens every year at this time. I told her I might just possibly stay here right through the winter. Anna got quite worked up about it.

'But that's never happened before', she said.

'Then it will happen this year', I replied.

'But', she objected, shaking her head, 'when something's always been done in a particular way?' 'Anna, dear', I said, 'there are going to be many other things that have never happened before. How old are you? Sixty? Who knows, you might even be here to see them happen.'

Of course, she can have had no idea what I was referring to. The French Revolution, that's in 1789, isn't it? There are a few dates I can remember. So Anna could be around when it happens, and I presume the news will reach us here. It's actually quite good that I'm not too well up in history, otherwise the temptation to play the prophet would be even greater. (And be regarded as a witch. That's no joke here, where we're obviously still in the Middle Ages. Only recently, Josefa told me, two young girls were burnt in Granada.)

Yesterday evening we had some music. It was the first time I have decided anything, a personal initiative. Otherwise, until now I have just been living out my 'predecessor's' unfinished life: I've worn her clothes (I still am wearing them, of course), eaten the things she liked (apart from the pig's testicles), taken my meals at the usual times, been to events she was invited to. I even feel the emotions that, sometime or other, have come to roost in her heart. But that's not what I want to write to you about just now. As far as the general course of my existence here is concerned, I have drifted along in the current of *her* life; anything else would have been impossible. But just a minute! There is something I decided, how could I forget. I replaced Anna, the old Dueña, with Josefa. In my first few days here I wasn't even consciously aware of what I'd done. (Perhaps that was why it didn't immediately occur to me just now.) It was a revolution, an upheaval that turned the whole house upside down. Now, today, when I know much more about what is going on around me, I would probably not dare to cause such an upheaval. A good thing I did it right away.

*I* decided we'd have some music. This evening I'd like some music, I told Josefa. I had good reason: I wanted to entertain the Conde. I didn't want to give him the opportunity to talk to me very much, firstly because I'm sure my accent, which I still have, will not sound Spanish to him, but strange, perhaps Russian or Tartar or something, and secondly, just because. He was a friend of the Duke's. Who knows what he's after here?

We dined. They have their evening meal late here, never

before ten or half past. The musicians had already arrived before dinner, accompanied by the music master, Maese Perdez. He appears to be in my employment, but since I have never seen him until now, I assume he doesn't live here in the palace, which I am naturally quite happy with. Perhaps he lives in our town house in Granada, perhaps he is not *my* music master alone, but is in service with other families at the same time? *One* family alone wouldn't occupy his time enough, probably not pay him enough, either. I can't ask him straight out. I can't ask too many questions to which the people here will assume I ought to know the answer. I just asked, Maese Perdez, where do you play the organ? At the church of the Franciscans, he replied, I did tell your Grace. Oh, of course, I'll be forgetting my own name next . . . But I can't use my poor memory as an excuse too often.

Maese Perdez is a tall man with a face so broad, it's not so much a face, more an expanse of skin. He wears a wig like everyone here, but also, and this is something I haven't seen on any other man since I arrived, a moustache, an ugly ginger moustache. A wig and a moustache together looks funny. I've never thought about it before, you just accept it when you see old pictures and engravings, but it was only Frederick the Great's sergeants who wore a wig and a moustache, wasn't it? And my music master, Perdez. Perhaps he thinks it looks artistic?

He walks in a peculiar way. He has what you might call an explicit gait. He places his feet on the ground gently but deliberately, and almost bows with every step, beating the air with his arms as if he were about to fly off. I assume he thinks it is graceful.

He brought two musicians from Granada with him, a flautist and a cellist. One of the servants here played the viola, and Maese Perdez himself the cembalo. I asked what it was they were playing, since I assume you'll be interested. Maese Perdez was very flattered by this expression of interest. They were playing sonatas for flute, viola, cello and cembalo by a composer I have never ever heard of. If I understood correctly he is a Catalan called Luis Misón. The first sonata was quite pretty, but the following eleven were – I wouldn't quite say boring, but very thorough. Twelve sonatas, and every one for the flute! But it's probably my fault for not being very musical. (If a musical person, like Wolfgang* for example, were here instead of me, do you think he would miss modern music which, by the very nature of things, he wouldn't be able to listen to here? Richard Strauss or Debussy? There wouldn't even be Schubert or Beethoven or Mozart, who must be how old? Five, and a long way from here in Salzburg. Someone like Wolfgang could just sit down and write everything he knew, but which hasn't been written yet; the *Rosenkavalier*, for example – but that would probably be going too far.) Twelve flute sonatas, then; occasionally the viola had a little solo passage, but the cello and cembalo were just accompaniment. I had the feeling that Conde Almaviva wasn't listening at all.

We dined during the twelve flute sonatas. Afterwards I ordered more music because I had realised that the Conde was determined to talk to me. I pretended I was engrossed in the music. I asked them about those pieces as well. They were sonatas by Maestro Pugnani, a Piedmontese who is the last word in Paris at the moment, and any last word in Paris is parrotted with gay abandon here. The sonatas only appeared last year, six of them, Opus 1. Maese Perdez played the violin, the cellist stuck to his cello, but the flautist was now playing the cembalo. There were only six sonatas. After the sixth I quickly held out my hand to the Count for him to kiss, and withdrew. Since then I haven't seen him again, but he's still here, Josefa told me.

Friday, 10th October

I don't know why I don't just go home. That's a silly thing to write, I know very well why I don't put on the ring, go to bed and return home. I know. The reason is not because if

---

* Here my sister is referring to a friend of mine from school, an excellent pianist, the musical prodigy of our old school; she often used to listen to him playing and talking about music when he visited me.

Ferdinand – my other Ferdinand, my husband here is a Ferdinand, too, of course – if Ferdinand and everyone else find my disappearance completely inexplicable, then my return will be even more inexplicable. Would I have to go to the police? Is it a crime or something? Do you already assume I'm dead? Has someone inherited my estate? Or has time passed more quickly here than there, as it does in a dream? I often wonder whether an hour here is an hour there. Perhaps only one second has gone since I disappeared, perhaps no time at all; perhaps Ferdi's still sleeping the sleep of the just. But that's not the reason. It's not that I might have problems when I come back. There are things here which I can't help. In my marriage – my marriage *there*, in your century – I have not been guilty of the slightest infidelity, not in deed, or word, or thought, not even to the extent of playing with the idea of the thought. I must admit that in recent years our marriage has not exactly throbbed with passion, but Ferdi was (I'm already writing 'was'; it gives me a bit of a shock, but I'll leave it, I want you to see my involuntary thoughts as well) someone you can respect. I have had nothing but good from him and I have come to find him not disagreeable physically. A marriage like many others. How can I help it if here feelings have been implanted in me which I don't want – didn't want; God! I *do* want them now, but I didn't ask for them. Just as I know what is in secret drawers here without having to look, so I can see into the heart of this woman, who I now have to be. Is it now my heart? Yes, it is my heart. I am guilty, because I knew before I came here. *Knew* is perhaps wrong . . .

There's no point in pursuing such legal or moral ideas (or am I already in the realm of theology?), when it's all so simple. I can no longer live in a time where he is not; not yet, anyway. I have sworn an oath to myself that I will go back after I have seen him again. I want to talk to him once, just one single time. Is that too much to ask? I don't know what his voice sounds like yet. But afterwards I'll go back. I think the other Stephanie owes me that, after all, it is her murder I'm helping to cover up.

I also know why she killed him. I can understand her.

Should I say I would have done it too? It's like living in a dream. Another silly thing to say. You don't need me to tell you it's like living in a dream. Perhaps it is a dream. Or perhaps my other life, the one in which you were my brother, is the dream? Dreamed by this Stephanie here? There was a book you once gave me. I can't remember the title, all I can remember is a place where someone says you can dream inside another dream, that dreams can be like the stories of a house, one above the other, and that you can wake up from a lower dream in a higher one, but waking up is still only a dream, and nobody knows whether he is really alive or just dreaming. What is truth? Nobody has ever written or said anything which hasn't been rejected by others as a lie. What is truth, then? Is reality true?

My God, why does it have to happen to *me*? This stupid ring. I remember when Ferdi gave it me on our tenth wedding anniversary I knew right away that I had seen it somewhere before. It's Estefanía's wedding ring. Did you realise that? Has it been looking for me? Has it been making its way down the centuries with the express aim of finding *me*? Another Stephanie with another Ferdinand? Who might not live in Granada, but at least in G-d-a-? And that Great-aunt Helen used to live here, of all things . . . Did the ring use her life here and her strange death in order to meet me? Like the soldier in the air-raid shelter?*

---

* Here Stephanie is referring to an incident from our childhood. It must have been in 1943, perhaps 1944. We were already living out in the country where it was somewhat safer, but now and then we used to go to visit our grandparents who, against our mother's wishes, had stayed in the flat in the city. The old folks refused to move, they believed the bombs wouldn't hurt two harmless old people like them, presumably because they were doing nothing to hurt the bomber pilots. Later, but that was early in 1945, my mother literally grabbed them by the collar and threw the two old people, kicking and screaming, out of the house. It was actually destroyed by bombs some time later, but at the time I'm speaking of, in 1943 or 1944, our grandparents were still living in the city. Stephanie and I, and, I think, our sister Isolde, were staying with our grandparents for a couple of days when there was – of course – an air-raid and we had to go down into the shelter in the cellar. I found it extremely interesting and was disap-

pointed that my grandmother refused to let me pop up to the street during the raid like my grandfather, who used all sorts of excuses to go up again. Grandfather was very obstinate. Just as, later on, he would cross when the lights were red, puffing at his pipe, so now he strolled round the city during the air-raids. He thought it wasn't his job to avoid the bombs, but rather that it was the bombs that should be making sure they didn't land on him.

Down in the cellar there was a violent debate going on between the very devout, not to say rabidly religious, owner of the house, a very fat lady who had two, if not three, fur coats on over her nightdress – not because of the cold, but to save them if the worst came to the worst – and a local minor Party official, the Nazi *Zellenleiter* Derendinger. What odd names we lumber our memories with for the rest of our lives! The Nazi *Zellenleiter* lived in the same house, one storey below my grandparents, and, in contrast to my grandfather, was a complete coward. Perhaps he thought that, as a key pillar of the Nazi Fatherland, the enemy pilots would have it in for him personally. In spite of that, my grandfather told me that Derendinger always arrived late in the air-raid shelter, long after the alarm had been given, and the reason was his uniform. Everyone else wore the bare essentials, the fat house-owner with her three fur coats over her nightdress for example, only Derendinger insisted on decking himself out in full *Zellenleiter* uniform, and that, given the boots and belts, swastika arm-band, shoulder-straps and decorations, was not such a simple matter, and was not made any simpler by the fact that he must have been quivering like an aspen leaf as he fastened the buttons and belts.

That evening too Derendinger had arrived in the cellar pretty late. We could already hear the detonation of the bombs as they landed, fortunately in distant parts of the town. Immediately Derendinger ordered the candle to be blown out. The pious landlady had lit the candle because it had been consecrated. Our Nazi said consecrated or not, it still used up oxygen and had to be blown out. The landlady said the house had belonged to her since it had been built and Derendinger was only a tenant and she could burn candles for as long as she wanted to. Derendinger was about to invoke the full authority of his uniform, when the house-owner had the idea of hanging the signed portrait of Hitler, which Derendinger had brought down into the cellar, on a nail in the wall and placing the candle in front of it. The consecrated candle was burning, she said, so that nothing would happen to their beloved Führer, and if Derendinger blew it out, she would tell the *Ortsgruppenleiter*.

The candle was left burning.

But then the whole affair began to lose its funny side as the sound of the bombs came nearer.

With us in the cellar was a soldier from the front who happened to be spending his leave with relatives in the house. He was a young man of twenty-one or twenty-two and rather ugly. He sat in a corner the whole

There is one thing I do know: whichever 'Life is a Dream' – for a change that's a quotation which is not an anachronism –, whether this life or the other one, whether both or neither, I will not return until I've seen him again.

Of course, Count Almaviva eventually managed to corner me. I couldn't avoid it, he made a formal request for an interview, on Monday before he left.

We sat beside a brazier in the room with the floral mosaic. I was on my guard. I'll have to be even more on my guard. The Count didn't waste much time on the polite preliminaries, but came straight to the matter which concerned him and which is doubtless the reason why he made the journey here from Seville.

'His Grace, the Duke, has been away for some time', he said.

'Yes', I said.

'For a surprisingly long time', he said.

'Since the 17th September', I said.

'Today is the 6th October', he said.

---

time and said nothing. Perhaps it was the presence of this gaunt, much-abused soldier that stopped Derendinger, who was much older and belonged to the category of what my grandfather called 'home-front layabouts', from laying down the law too much.

A bomb exploding close by shook the house to its foundations (the next day we saw the row of houses that had been flattened a couple of streets away). We could hear the tinkle of glass and the crackle of shrapnel. The young soldier went to one of the doors and opened it slightly, why we shall never know, since a piece of shrapnel no more than the size of a man's thumb struck him in the middle of his forehead and killed him instantly.

It's this soldier Stephanie is referring to. At the front he had survived many dangers, many grenades had flown past without harming him, but in the cellar of a house that was almost completely undamaged in the raid he was hit by a piece of shrapnel which – we reconstructed its path later from the marks it had made on the walls – must have taken a very complicated route through doors and windows and certainly did not have enough force left to penetrate the iron door, though still sufficient for the young man's forehead. And it was he himself who had made the tiny opening in the door, the last obstacle to the projectile that was to kill him.

'The shrapnel sought him out', was what our grandmother said.

Superfluous to say that grandfather returned from his stroll unharmed.

'That is correct, Count', I said, 'it is the 6th October precisely, and', I added, since the calendar, which I had been reading, lay open on the table before me, 'the feast of St. Bruno of Cologne, the founder of the Carthusian order.'

The Count gave me a suspicious look. I realised I would have to be more careful.

'His Grace has never been away hunting for so long before', he said.

'Not as far as I can remember', I said. It was the truth.

'We are concerned about his Highness', he said.

'So am I', I said. In a certain way, that was true as well. 'Who is this 'we'?'

'His friends', he said.

'You and the Chevalier de Florimonte!'

'And the Chaplain, Don Gonzalo.'

'Where is the Chevalier at the moment?'

'As far as I know', said the Count, 'he has gone to Madrid.'

'Oh, he has, has he?'

'Your Grace', he said, 'there is no alternative. You must tell us where the Duke is.'

'I would, with pleasure, if I only knew', I said.

'Who else would know?'

'You know as well as I, Count Almaviva, that the Duke often used to go away without telling me where, and you know the reason, too, I think.'

'But your Grace . . .'

'What you mean to say is that it is the first time he has gone away without informing *you*?'

'Don't forget, your Grace, that we are close friends.'

'You are wondering why he didn't tell you, then. Well, you'll have to ask him, not me.'

'Your Grace, I must tell you that the matter has already led to repercussions.'

'What matter?'

'The disappearance of the Duke. It's not every day that a Duke disappears. His Grace, the Archbishop, was extremely concerned.'

'What concern is it of the Archbishop's?'

'His Grace is one of the foremost people in Granada. Naturally it is of concern to the Archbishop.'

'And how does the Archbishop come to know that my husband has disappeared?'

'The whole of Granada is talking of nothing else.'

'And how do you know that the Archbishop is concerned?'

'I have talked to him.'

'Aha, you've talked to him. About the Duke's disappearance? And why? Is it any concern of yours?'

'We are friends, your Grace . . .'

'And has the Chevalier de Florimonte talked to the Archbishop as well?'

'No, only the Chaplain . . .' From the way he suddenly broke off I realised that was something he would have preferred not to have said.

'And when was that, if I may ask?'

'Last Wednesday.'

'The Chaplain was not good enough to inform me.'

'It wasn't a very important conversation . . .'

'Important enough for you to talk about it, Count.'

'Your Grace, one can't just let the matter rest.'

'What should I do? Send out a search party for the Duke?'

'It is impossible that you don't know where the Duke is.'

'But I do not know.'

'A Duke cannot just disappear into thin air.'

'Then you know more than I do. Perhaps you do know more than I. Perhaps *I* ought to be asking *you* where the Duke is. Should I ask you where the Duke was last August? Last June? In the spring? (I chose the months at random. There was no risk in doing so, since the Duke was almost permanently 'out hunting' with his cronies.)

'But he has never before been away for three weeks', said the Count.

'And never on his own, you mean. Well, perhaps he's changed his habits. How should I know? You'll have to ask him.'

'We've been to the hunting lodge . . .'

'I know that you were good enough to check it, even before I had the opportunity of asking you to do so. You didn't find him?'

'Your Grace', said the Count, 'it is getting beyond a joke. He might have had an accident.'

'Naturally the thought has already occurred to me', I said, 'although, as you can imagine, I try to avoid it.'

'There are all sorts of riff-raff around, especially since the war started and the army was withdrawn from the area. He might have been attacked.'

'Can I do anything about it?'

'His Grace, the Archbishop was very concerned, and above all very surprised that your Grace is behaving as if nothing had happened.'

'I cannot help it if the Archbishop is surprised. So far nothing has happened except that someone – a someone of the highest rank, I agree – who was not always as courteous as he might have been towards his wife, has decided to go away without saying where. I can assure you, Count, that he clearly did not have the opportunity of saying goodbye to me.'

'I had hoped for more from this conversation, your Grace', he said.

'I cannot tell you more than I know, Count Almaviva.'

He stood up. Perhaps the next thing I said was not a good idea, but how else was I to find out his name?

'Tell me something, Count, something completely different. You were at the requiem for her late Majesty, weren't you?'

'I had that honour.'

'Who was the gentleman . . .', I described him, trying to speak as casually as I could.

'But your Grace must know your own cousin?'

'So that's who . . .' I'm afraid my embarrassment was all too visible, 'my cousin, yes, of course. I have so many cousins. I haven't seen him for such a long time. it would have been very embarrassing if I'd had to ask one of my relations. I haven't seen him for ages.'

'Of course not, since he lives in Malta.'

'In Malta? On the island?'

'Where else, since he's a Knight of the Order of Malta.'

'I've a memory like a sieve! A Knight of Malta. Of course. May I wish you a safe journey?'

That, roughly, was the conversation. I think I have written it down more or less word for word. I don't doubt that the whole of Granada is talking of the disappearing Duke. I can't quite see what's behind it, but clearly the three rogues, the Chaplain, the shady Chevalier and the dapper Count met in Granada and discussed what to do. Perhaps they are under suspicion themselves? So they sent the Chevalier to Madrid? To whom? To the Minister? To the King? They've been whispering in the Archbishop's ear. Perhaps I should get Josefa to find me a gorge up there in the woods and we could drop the Duke's body into it? So that it would look as if it might have been bandits? I would never have thought of that but for what the Count said. It won't be very pleasant taking the Duke out of the cupboard, I can well imagine what state the corpse will be in by now. But what can I do? Should I do anything at all? Is there anyone I can turn to for advice? There's no one.

But I will ask Josefa to tell me the name of the cousin who's a Knight of Malta.

Thursday, 18th November

I haven't written to you for over a month, but what does it matter since you won't get this letter, if at all, until two hundred years from now.

We have moved into the town. It was unavoidable. I wouldn't have known how to make staying out there plausible. It would have been unheard of for a lady of my rank to spend the winter in the country. And anyway, it was getting rather uncomfortable out there. It's a summer palace and more or less impossible to heat. The palace here in Granada is equipped for winter, and the winter can be cold, even here in Andalusia. We don't have any snow, of course, except in the distance, up on the Mulhacén, but you don't have to look at it. However, it does rain quite a lot and the wind blows, and it's cold when it comes whistling down from the mountain.

It was around the 15th October that we moved into the town. Anna suggested I should leave Josefa out there, so there'd be someone to look after the place. All I replied was that I had already thought of it, of leaving someone out there to look after the place, that is, but that I was more inclined to the view that she, Anna, should be given the honour of such a responsible task. After that she naturally shut up and spent the rest of her time scurrying around in silence, supervising the complexities of the removal. For days on end various servants rode or drove into town and then back out again with carts or pack-horses, transporting crates and cases. God knows what multitude of things had to be taken, but Anna was so pleased that we were actually going that she saw to everything herself.

The move brought new problems for me. That I did not know the town house, my own town house, was the least of them. Basically I just had to let Josefa go on in front, and there I was, in my rooms.

But how will things work with the bedroom? I've brought the ring with me, of course, I took it out of the secret compartment in the writing desk along with my jewelry and the gold coins, over two hundred of them. Here I've found another writing desk that also has a secret compartment, and that's where I've stowed everything. But what will happen when I have to leave? All I know is that I have to put the ring on, lie down in the bed out there and go to sleep. But what will happen if I do that in this bed here? Where will I wake up then?

I have a very odd feeling, as if I were living in a bottomless space with endless ropes running across it, a dense network of ropes. I once had a dream like that. Everywhere I look, above me, below me, to the left, to the right, there are ropes stretched across making strange rectangles and hexagons, fairly small ones, but not so small that you couldn't fall through. I feel safe and at the same time unsafe. There's no point in climbing up, since there's no end in sight. It's not dangerous to fall down, you would get caught somewhere. A quiet, eerie world, with strange perspectives all around. It's rather similar to when you stand between two mirrors.

Where will I end up if I drop into the receding dream here in the town house?

I'll move back out to the palace as soon as at all possible. Josèfa said the other great families usually move back to the country in the middle of March, so I'll go on the 1st March.

I'm afraid of having to go back – and I don't mean going back to the summer residence. It's not that I'm afraid of what I will find there, it's the journey itself I'm afraid of. I've always been afraid of narrow passages and low caves. On the journey you crawl along a tube that gets narrower and narrower. What use is it that you can see the dull light of another day shimmering far, far away on the other side, when in the middle, at the place where the stone vats of time weigh down upon it, the passage becomes so narrow that you have to crawl and can scarcely move your arms. At the very thought I feel as if I'm suffocating, and yet one day I will have to pass through it. Yesterday I received a letter which made it plain that things will not go on as calmly as they have up to now.

I'll tell you about the letter later.

It was the 14th October when we left the palace out there, though everything was so chaotic, it could well have been the 13th.

Do you know how painful fire can be? I do. Of course, you never have a real fire. You have banished fire behind steel walls, to stoves, to central heating plants. In your world fire burns unseen, you've done away with it, like sin or the sight of death; for you, fire means disaster. You don't know the benefits of fire any more, or at most indirectly, when the central heating breaks down. You have a very indirect life in general.

But fire can be painful. No cut or blow or wound is as unutterably painful as a burn. Our fire was not a disaster. On the contrary. Josefa and I lit it ourselves.

We couldn't conceal the fact that we had been out for a

ride. (Side-saddle, an awfully stupid arrangement, but a necessary one when you remember what I told you about women here wearing nothing under their skirts; without a doubt to ride properly like that would be even more uncomfortable.) We didn't take the coach because then we would have had to take a coachman. We wanted to be alone. We said we were going to ride to a pilgrimage chapel to make some kind of vow. Whether Anna and the Chaplain believed us, I don't know.

We set off after breakfast. I'm not sure I would have known how to ride here if I hadn't insisted on taking a few riding lessons in my former existence, in your world.

The middle of October here is still late summer. Everything is yellow or light brown, when the weather's bad the sky is a dull violet colour. We rode out a long way, into what they call a forest here. (Josefa, by the way, took two pairs of loaded pistols.) The hunting lodge is on a high plateau which is covered to a roughly equal extent with boulders and stunted trees, though more likely they're dwarf pines. The plateau looks like the back of a sleeping dragon. On all sides the view is blocked by mountains that look as if they're formed of lava or ash, up above is the violet sky. I think it was more her mount than Josefa herself that found the way to the lodge. I hope it can find the way back, I kept saying. It will, Josefa said.

The hunting lodge, an astonishingly elegant building for an inhospitable high plateau like this, lies in a dip between two ridges where a stream, which has long since dried up, gouged out its course in the yellow soil. The tumbledown old stable is a hundred yards further on.

We had been riding for two hours and, if you'll excuse my mentioning it, my backside was completely numb. 'Why', Josefa asked me during the ride, 'did your Grace kill the Duke?'

Had I not thought about the matter until then, or did the sudden question make the answer – that is, the knowledge I held that made an answer possible – burst within me, just as a boil bursts?

'Don't you know?' I asked.

'I can imagine', said Josefa, 'more or less.'

'And?'

'He was . . .', she hesitated, 'a bad lot.'

'He was very bad.'

'He tried it on with me as well', said Josefa.

'You as well?'

'Naturally. They tried it on with all of us, the Duke, the Count, the Chevalier as he calls himself, and the Chaplain. though the Chaplain likes watching best.'

'And were they – successful?'

'With me?'

'Yes?'

'What you have to realise, your Grace, is that they like things easy as well. They weren't very keen on having to make an effort, giving presents and persuading people, having to wait and things like that. If you didn't make it easy for them, they left you in peace. There were enough who did make it easy for them.'

'I couldn't stand it any longer, Josefa', I said.

'That I can well imagine, your Grace.'

'No, no. Not his affairs. At least he still had the grace to use the excuse that he was going out hunting.'

'You mean because of Don Felix?' Don Felix is the Knight of Malta.

'No, not because of Don Felix, actually.'

'Wasn't his Grace, the Duke, jealous of Don Felix?'

'He wouldn't have had any reason to be jealous.'

'When a man wants to, he can always find a reason to be jealous.'

'Don Felix is a Knight of the Sovereign Order of St. John of Malta, Josefa, that means he is in holy orders.'

'Is there anything more powerful to move a woman's heart than the fact that a man is not to be had, not for love nor money, as the saying goes? The fact that he belongs to another woman, that's nothing, but that he's beyond your reach, has gone away, never to return, that he's far above you or far below you, that he's dead or, why not, that he's a Knight of the Sovereign Order of St. John of Malta. Just a priest, that's not enough. In the first place priests nowadays are all more or less randy as goats, and secondly, they have such a capon look about them. Their dress is more like women's clothes than men's clothes. Can you imagine, your Grace, being . . . that one of them should lift up his cassock and . . .'

'Josefa!'

'A Knight of Malta, on the other hand, he's an officer. You forget he's a priest, you have to keep reminding yourself. Like Don Felix – how old might he be?'

'Thirty-two.' (I had been making enquiries.)

'Thirty-two and so serious! He'll only talk to his own kind, women will just be so much vermin to him.'

'No, that's not true. Vermin can be dangerous. Don Felix always behaves with the greatest courtesy; the courtesy of a man to whom women are no danger.'

'He slaps his sword against his leg when he's reading his breviary', Josefa went on dreamily. 'Have you seen his legs?'

'It's much too sad a business, Josefa dear, for me to be always thinking about his legs.'

'So why did you kill his Grace?'

'I offered him a separation, a very discreet separation, of course. I told him he might suddenly feel like going out hunting in the middle of the night, for example, or he might want to come home from hunting in the middle of the night, and would be prevented because he didn't want to disturb my sleep. I offered, no, I begged him to let me sleep in a separate bedroom.'

'That would have been giving tacit approval to all his philandering.'

'It would have, but I don't think he understood. I don't know why, but he insisted we stay in the same bedroom.'

'Did he . . .'

'No, after that he never touched me again.'

'He wanted to torment you.'

'That is true. Every night before we went to sleep he would tell me he was going to kill me. That night – or in a month's time – or the day after tomorrow . . . how long can a person put up with that, Josefa?'

'One night at the most.'

'I put up with it for six months.'

'Did his Grace really mean it?'

'He was much too stupid to say anything he didn't mean seriously.'

Josefa rode beside me, silent.

'Didn't you know all this?'

'There were rumours, your Grace.'

'Wouldn't you have killed him?'

'Probably much, much sooner, your Grace. My God!' She hit the horse with her riding-crop.

'Josefa, it's not the horse's fault.'

'It's a stallion', she said.

There was no one left in the hunting lodge. We knew that already. We didn't waste any time, we went straight to the stable where the cupboard with the Duke's corpse had been put.

'Do you think we should see if there's anything else in there it would be a pity to burn?' I asked.

'Why bother', she said, 'there's nothing but rubbish.'

We knelt down at one corner where we were out of the wind and started striking sparks into the tinderbox.

'Won't they see the fire down in the valley?' I asked.

'What if they do, your Grace?'

Making a fire with flint and tinder is a very laborious process. Finally we got the kindling burning. Josefa threw it into the hut, but it did not set it alight. It took three bundles before the door started burning, but then the whole thing went up in flames. In no time at all the old stable was ablaze, the beams were cracking and crashing to the floor so that the sparks flew all around.

I wanted to go and see if the cupboard was burning as well. That's how I found out how painful fire can be. You can force yourself to stand in cold water for a while, or hold a lump of ice in your hand. If someone bites your finger, just where the nails join the skin, you can still bear it by gritting your teeth, but fire spreads a shield of unbelievable pain around it, pain that immediately penetrates your every pore, so that you just have to move back. If you can. I had to think of the two girls they burned in Granada last September because they thought they were witches. They couldn't move back. It's not the devils flying out of the witches that scream, it's the witches themselves. And you can't say anything, especially if you're a woman, or they'll think your a witch yourself. Living at a time when you can be burnt at the stake, that's something else we're not used to, you and I.

The hut burnt down pretty quickly once it had started. We couldn't actually see whether the cupboard had burnt too, but the intensity of the fire was such that there can't have been anything left at all. We rode back down and were home before the angelus. Naturally the fire had been seen from the valley, but people thought it was a campfire lit by the bandits who are all over the place round here, though we didn't see any during our ride.

Thus I discharged my last liability before I moved to the town house here, and already there's another one in the offing. It hasn't actually appeared yet, but it's on the horizon: Don Fernando de I., the son of the cousin of the late Duke. He's written to me. He is the heir apparent to the title and has announced his arrival from Madrid. I can imagine what he wants.

The letter arrived yesterday.

### The Feast of the Presentation of the Blessed Virgin in Jerusalem

The feast of the Presentation of the Virgin, *festum praesentationis Mariae*, is a holiday here. No one works. The things you learn. You could have beat me senseless, brother dear, but while I still lived in your time, I would not have been able to tell you that the 21st November is the *festum praesentationis Mariae*. But here everyone knows. Josefa, and not only Josefa, the lowliest of my stableboys will rattle off the feasts of the Virgin and that kind of thing in his sleep if you ask him. It has nothing to do with education. How many feast days have we not had since I have been here: *Teresa de Jesus, virgo seraphica* – on the 15th October, I think, at least on the day before we moved to the town house (in that case it would have been the 16th when we moved, and not the 14th as I wrote recently); All Saints' Day is a feast day of course, All Souls' too, on the 2nd November, and then on the 3rd there's a local feast in honour of Our Lady. Add to those the birthdays of the King, the Queen, various Infantes, the Pope, the Cardinal, and all in all I think that even though Saturday counts as a normal working day right up to the evening, worked out over the whole year they must have less than a forty-eight-hour week here. So it's nothing to do with education if the stableboy can recite the feasts of the Virgin in his sleep, it's a matter of what you might call legal holiday entitlement.

And you don't count the days in the same way – 21st November, 22nd November, and so on – you say, 'on the Sunday after All Saints' Day' or, 'on the Tuesday in the first week of Advent'. On the Tuesday in the first week of Advent my cousin, Don Fernando de I., is going to return to Madrid, or so he told me yesterday evening. That means he's hardly going to stay a fortnight. Why was that more or less the first thing he told me, he hardly waited until he'd finished kissing my hand? Either he wanted to reassure me, to tell me that I wouldn't have to put up with him for too long, or he wanted to suggest that he was prepared to deal with the matter – for which he's come all the way from Madrid – speedily, within two weeks; that's incredibly fast for a Spaniard, you might even say: overhasty.

At first he was somewhat put out. But can I help it if he didn't make sure he knew where I was beforehand? He'd already been to Granada, yesterday, and then he rode out to our summer residence with his shabby retinue, found no one there and had to ride back to Granada.

He felt it incumbent upon him to tell me straight away that the people out there were still talking about the fire in the hills. A couple of the bolder peasant lads had gone up and seen that it was the old stable by the hunting lodge that had burnt down. Probably the work, he went on, of those bandits everyone was talking about. I put on a show of indignation and ordered someone – I gave Anna the task of seeing to it – to go and see if everything was in order in the hunting lodge. In the meantime, however, the snow has arrived up there, so we won't be able to check before the spring. I'm quite happy with that.

Don Fernando is as fat as a barrel. I've never met anyone in my life before who stinks as much as he does. It's a well known fact that hardly anyone ever washes here. We were taught at school, I think, that there wasn't a single bathtub in the whole of the Palace of Versailles. It was probably true and they are even less likely to have bathtubs here. They're completely unknown. If I want to wash, Josefa brings a wooden tub and hot water, I step into it and she washes me down with a sponge. (This was something in which the Chaplain, Don Gonzalo, was most interested. He asked Josefa about it a couple of times, in confidence, and got her to describe the procedure in detail. A few times already he's tried to talk to me while I was being washed – we could put up a little screen, he said –, on the grounds that he had something of immense importance to tell me. I refused to allow it, of course.) Josefa on the other hand is extremely worried at all this washing. It harms the skin, she says.

Don Fernando seems to have dispensed with washing entirely. (Perhaps I'll offend him by having a tub of hot water sent up to his room, as a polite gesture, of course.) He smells of – you can well imagine what he smells of, especially given that he's so fat. Sometimes I feel he's going rancid. And his breath – he hardly has any teeth left. Almost everyone here, if they're a little older, have lost most of their teeth. 'A little older' means over thirty. Ah, the good old days. Anna has none left at all, of course, Count Almaviva has three upper front teeth missing, and the rest are pretty black. The Chaplain was complaining recently that he had lost his last tooth. It's not unusual in company (recently I was invited to take chocolate with the Marquesa de F., who seems to be a cousin of mine) for people to spend hours talking about teeth, teeth they still have, or teeth they've just lost.

You sometimes hear people say this or that is not the way the man in the street imagines it to be. I'm not well up enough in the various sciences to know which things are, or are not, the way the ordinary or uneducated person imagines, but since I've been living here I do know that the 18th century is precisely the way the man in the street imagines it would be. A rancid atmosphere, overlaid with sickly-sweet perfume (Don Fernando uses perfume of course); priest-ridden old women of both sexes who, out of snobbery, flirt with a sham enlightenment. An unbearably musty century, perhaps especially so here in Spain. If it weren't for the music – here in Granada, where it's more convenient, I have them play for me every day; I've sent for the latest scores from Paris, and some should be arriving from Vienna any day now – if it weren't for the be-all and end-all of our century, music, which is not only thriving, but living and breathing, all-inspiring, everywhere seething, binding each to all, it would be impossible to live in this century. Music is an escape, of course. People here escape into music. People are crazy for anything new in music. (Are they like that in your time? No.) There is hardly anyone who can't play an instrument, whether duchess or stableboy. Everyone can sing. I have a scullion, a tenor, who sings – your opera houses would be drooling over him. I have commissioned a cantata for him from the *Kapellmeister* of the local cathedral. Josefa, for example, plays the cembalo as well as anyone could desire. The Chaplain, however disagreeable I may find him personally, plays the viola da gamba exceptionally well, but doesn't like to play because Alejandro, the servant, plays it even better. To my shame I must confess that I have heard both and cannot tell the difference. I have begun taking lessons on the harp. Music wherever you look. There are composers galore, and yet they can scarcely keep up with the demand for new compositions, so great it is. We can listen to and play music everywhere, we float on music, we cannot get enough music.

Naturally I've thought about the reasons. In the first place, as I said before, it's an escape. Nothing can touch you in music. Music is not political, neither one thing nor the other, neither Catholic, nor Protestant. It is unthinkable that a Catholic prince would employ a Protestant as personal physician. But last year, the Chevalier de Florimonte knew of it, of course, a Protestant was appointed organist at Milan Cathedral, and no one thought anything about it. He's said to be called Bach. A relative of Johann Sebastian?*

But there's another thing about this music: the taste of the musical public is precisely in tune with what is modern. Has that been true of other periods? I don't know. In the time in which you are living things are certainly different. As far as I can tell it will soon be different here, perhaps it will already have changed in twenty years time.

Music: the vent through which the only fresh air comes into this musty, over-perfumed century. The revolution *must* come. Things can't go on like this much longer. There is one thing that is comforting, perhaps even exciting: if you listen carefully you can hear the rustling of a new age. The butterfly hasn't emerged from the chrysalis yet, but it's already wriggling and pushing and pumping inside its pupa. Comforting for the people here, not for me; I know it will be a black butterfly, a death's head. The sun of liberalism, of true, genuine liberalism, has cast a streak of silver along the horizon which we can see here and now, but it will have set before the people awake.

That is the 18th century just as the man in the street imagines it. And let me tell you, it wouldn't be earth-shattering, but I'm coming close to inventing the water-closet prematurely. The only thing that stops me doing it is that I might attract too much attention. The Inquisition is still no joking matter, and it could well be that they would regard something like that as witchcraft.

Don Fernando arrived with a retinue. In the first place

---

* I've looked him up. The Chevalier de Florimonte is right. In 1760 Johann Christian Bach, the youngest son of Johann Sebastian, was appointed cathedral organist in Milan, though only after he had converted to Catholicism. But even before that, as a Protestant, he composed masses and other church music, which was performed and printed, and no one thought anything of it.

there was his eldest son, a nose-picking oaf of about fourteen, then his valet, two servants, a chaplain and a few grooms. When you look at the whole crew, you have the impression he's invested all his reserves in it and gone round his friends and acquaintances as well, cap in hand, just to be able to arrive here in a manner befitting his rank and station. His servants have been stuffing themselves practically uninterruptedly since they've been here. They must have been half starved. The horses were mere skeletons, the only coach had broken springs. The whole company is down at heel and out at the elbows.

Moreover I have the impression that Don Fernando was not very keen to come here at all. Reading between the lines, it was obvious that his wife was the driving force behind the journey. In her clever way, Josefa pumped all his servants and grooms one after the other, and they prattled on about all sorts of things, the nub of which is that the only reason our old friend, the Chevalier de Florimonte, went – or, rather, was sent by Count Almaviva and my Chaplain – to Madrid at the end of September was to visit Don Fernando and tell him about the disappearance of the Duke. But the Chevalier made such a poor impression on Don Fernando, who is, after all, a *hidalgo*, if a rather stupid one, that he decided he was nothing but wind-bag and a charlatan. I can just imagine the Chevalier making his entrance, puffed up with self-importance. Don Fernando refused to believe a word of what he said – perhaps simply in order to avoid possible complications – and sent him packing. That was the end of September.

It must have been about the middle of October that the Chevalier arrived back in Granada, and then something must have happened, a fact which does not fill me with reassurance. Around the time when I was moving from our summer palace to the town house here, the three of them, the Conde, the Chaplain and the Chevalier, went to see the Archbishop. And the Archbishop sent a letter to Don Fernando, at which Don Fernando's wife nagged on at her fat husband until he agreed to make the journey to Granada.

What shall I do now? The Inquisition is no joking matter, as I have already said. But something like this does not fall into the remit of the Inquisition. At my instigation, Josefa made covert enquiries of a lawyer – not my own, of course. Such *casos de corte* are tried either by the assembly of the peers of the realm, *el consejo real*, or by the *cancillería de Granada*. I know it was perhaps a mistake to send Josefa to the lawyer, but I have to know from which direction danger will come.

Next Monday I'm giving a soirée for Don Fernando, on the occasion of the birthday of the Infanta, Maria Luisa, and the birthday of the late Queen, Maria Amalia. It'll be the first large party I've given. It will also be the first large party in this house at which the Duke will not be present. I am going to give instructions that the Chevalier de Florimonte is only to be admitted if he can produce impeccable documents attesting his noble birth. That he will scarcely be able to do.

Brief letter, Monday 24th

Everything's in chaos, tonight is the *soirée*. Anna has charge of the preparations; she's overjoyed, and is turning the whole house upside down. I've already had a tearful submission from the Chaplain, first thing this morning: in the short time allowed, the noble Chevalier de Florimonte cannot procure the documents I require. But the Chevalier is prepared to swear on the sacred host that his lineage is impeccable, with at least thirty-two quarterings.

I said that I did not doubt that the noble Chevalier would be prepared to swear any oath required of him, if it would gain him *entrée* to an aristocratic *soirée*. I, however, was insisting on documents. The Chevalier, replied the Chaplain, was inconsolable. I can well believe it. My *soirée* seems to be looked on as the high-point of the social season. If the Chevalier is not there, he'll be finished in Granada.

There's not a quiet spot in the house, apart from my bedroom and my boudoir, which they've had the goodness to exempt from the general chaos. Josefa packed me off here, she said I was to keep out of the way for an hour and have a lie down. But I'm not tired, quite the contrary, so I'm writing you this little letter. Even in here I can still hear the noise. Next door they're setting up a room where people can relieve themselves. Do you know what that is? A large room with chamber pots arranged along all four walls. That's it. I'll invent that water-closet after all. But, I asked Anna, aren't there at least two rooms, one for women to relieve themselves in, and another for men? Anna stared at me, wide-eyed. No, why on earth should there be? She'd never heard the like, one specially for the ladies, and one for the gentlemen.

Don Fernando finds his mission here most disagreeable. Needless to say, I do nothing to make it more agreeable. He found our first meeting not only disagreeable, but downright embarrassing. He sat there, fat and rancid-smelling, completely incapable of saying a single word.

It's obvious what his wife told him to do while he's here. He's to find out whether the Duke is dead, and if he is dead, he's to register his claim to the title with the College of Heralds, secure the inheritance to all houses and estates, and throw me out. What is also obvious to me is that the death of the Duke and the inheritance is the only way out of his predicament for Don Fernando. He is deep in debt and on his last legs, financially speaking. That's something else my clever Josefa wormed out of his servants, who, by now, have more or less eaten their fill.

His good lady will have made it very clear to him that he's not to return to Madrid without something to show for it. At the very least he will need a tangible hint of a prospect of the title to keep his creditors at bay for a few months longer. But of course, he can't tell me that to my face. His wife must be stupid too, she couldn't have chosen anyone less suited for a delicate mission like this than her own husband. But who else is there she could have sent?

'What can I do for you, cousin?' I asked.

He talked about the weather, so I talked about the weather too. He talked about his teeth, then about his wife's teeth, his parents-in-law's teeth, and from their teeth he moved on to the general state of health of his family, then to that of the King, the Infantes and the ambassadors of various foreign countries. The Archbishop of Toledo, they say, has only two teeth left, and any day one of them is likely to fall out.

Don Fernando's difficulty in bringing the conversation round to the Duke was all to obvious. He kept dropping hints, but I deliberately misunderstood them. Finally he took a deep breath and – doubtless with his wife's injunctions still ringing in his ear – asked, 'My cousin, the Duke, is he out hunting?'

'Yes', I replied.

'Since September, they say?'

'Since September', I said.

'That seems quite a long time.' He had to force the words out, and it was such an effort that he seemed to grow even fatter, almost bursting out of the chair he was sitting in. It was as if he were laying an egg.

'That is true', I said. 'Now you mention it, it does seem quite a long time.'

That was all. I feel he is grateful to me if I don't speak to him. And yet every day there's a letter for him from his wife in Madrid. It would be easy for Josefa to intercept one of them, but what would be the point of reading it? I can imagine what's in them.

Don Felix is coming to my *soirée* tonight.

4th December, midnight

His name is Don Enrique Fernandez Picaza y Escaramujo, he is about seventy years old and extremely polite. Although common sense tells me to err on the side of caution, I can't help feeling that Don Picaza is well-disposed towards me. He is a member of the Cancillería. At about five o'clock this afternoon he asked for an audience with me. I had a light taken into the library and a fire made.

'It is purely a matter of form, your Grace,' said Don Picaza, 'but matters of this importance cannot be allowed to take their own course. I assume your Grace was the last person to have seen his Grace, the Duke alive?'

'Will you permit me to ask a question, Don Picaza?'

'As many as you like, your Grace.'

'How do you know that the Duke has, let us say, disappeared?'

'The whole city is talking of nothing else.'

'I can hardly imagine', I said, 'that the mere fact that it is the talk of the town would lead such an august body as the Cancillería to investigate the matter.'

'You are right, your Grace, No, no, we are not moved by mere gossip. It was his Grace, the Archbishop, who informed us of the matter.'

'And when, if I might ask?'

'You may ask, of course you may, it is you who are most closely concerned, after all. It was on the 17th October that his reverend Grace –'

I was about to say something, but he forestalled me.

'I know what you are going to say. You are going to point out that today is the 4th December . . . You must realise that we members of the Cancillería are old men. I am one of the youngest. It is not our habit to rush things.'

'But you remember the date so precisely.'

'I am a lawyer, your Grace.'

This might be the place to add something else I have learnt in the meantime: Spanish lawyers are the most ridiculous in the world. Their studies consist of learning by rote and their examinations of reeling it off as quickly as possible. The one who can speak the quickest gets the best mark. I have heard of one lawyer in Seville whose voice simply ran away with him at the exam and he hasn't been able to stop since. He still talks unceasingly, even though he has all sorts of blisters on his lips and tongue.

However, all this learning by heart does mean that Spanish lawyers have good memories.

'I see', I said. 'You were asking whether I was the last person to see my husband. How should I know?'

'When did you last see him?'

'If you want the precise details, we, my husband and I that is, went to bed on the evening of the 16th September, a date I will remember for as long as I live. I went to sleep and when I woke up on the morning of the 17th September, he had gone.'

'He had expressed to you, your Grace, the intention of riding out to hunt?'

'To me he expressed no intention at all. Perhaps it is humiliating to have to admit it, but it was only when I questioned members of my household that I discovered that the Duke had gone out hunting.'

'But he didn't really ride out to hunt?'

'It's certainly true that he's never stayed out hunting so long before.'

'Do you suspect – do pardon me, your Grace, it's not easy to have to ask this kind of question . . .'

'I will help you. You want to ask me whether I suspect he is dead.'

'You are too kind, your Grace.'

'I have no opinion on that at all. What should I base an opinion on?'

'It has to be cleared up. The Duke is a great lord. He is a Grandee of the kingdom. His Majesty has already been informed of the matter. It is a *casus* with the most far-reaching implications. If a coachman or whatever should disappear, well . . . that happens quite often. But a Spanish Grandee can't just disappear without trace. The law doesn't provide for it. The matter will *have* to be cleared up.'

'The are various theories', I said. 'There are theories which a certain person was kind enough to elaborate in my own house. Either, so the theory goes, the Duke fell into a gorge while he was out hunting, for example, and broke his neck; or he was robbed and murdered by bandits, of which there are plenty around since war broke out.'

'In either case his corpse should have been found.'

'Probably, if there had been a search.'

'There has been a search, your Grace.'

'There has?'

'The Cancillería has not been idle in the time since the 17th October.'

'And where did the Cancillería make its search?'

'Everywhere, in the whole district.'

'And how does the Cancillería know how far the Duke rode?'

'The Duke rode nowhere at all. The Duke did not take a horse.'

'That is news to me. How do you know?'

'The Cancillería has not been idle since the 17th October.'

'I think it very unlikely that my husband would have gone hunting without a horse.'

'We also, your Grace', said Don Picaza. 'I'm afraid I must warn your Grace that, with all due consideration for you and your family, we, the Cancillería that is, have come to the conclusion that we are dealing with a – crime. We have sent a corresponding report to His Majesty.'

'Does it surprise you, Don Picaza, if I tell you that the same idea had occurred to me?'

'It does not surprise me, your Grace.'

'Don Picaza . . .'

'Yes, your Grace?'

'I'll offer a reward of one thousand *reales* for anyone who finds the murderer.'

'How much?'

'One thousand *reales*.'

One thousand *reales* is a small fortune. I don't know if it was a good idea to say that. It just suddenly came to me. If the Cancillería should harbour the suspicion that I . . . then at least it must make them question their suspicion if I offer such an outrageous sum as a reward. But would not the actual effect be to encourage my pursuers?

'You see . . . yes, Don Picaza, perhaps it is too soon for such a reward. I will offer the reward when it has been established that a crime has been committed. Basically we know nothing. I will offer the reward when the Duke's corpse has been found. But I thank you, Don Picaza, and the Cancillería for all your trouble.'

Don Picaza understood the audience was at an end, and stood up.

'One more thing, Don Picaza . . .' This, too, was a sudden

idea, but one that I am unreservedly proud of. 'Who is this Chevalier de Florimonte?'

'An Italian, as far as I know.'

'And that, I fear, is the only thing that is known about him. Recently he had been very intimate with the Duke. I have to admit that I myself did not find him very agreeable. At my little *soirée* a few days ago I allowed myself a little joke: I told the servants not to let him in unless he could produce impeccable proof of his aristocratic lineage. Not a scrap of proof did he produce, but that didn't stop him from slipping into the house through the kitchen and holding forth at my *soirée*.'

'I had heard of that . . .'

'So you do know him?'

'No, your Grace, all I have heard of is the, if you'll excuse the expression, amusing little incident. The whole town is talking about it.'

'Of that as well? And is that of interest to such an august body as the Cancillería too?'

'But your Grace, that is of interest to anyone who likes a good laugh.'

To put you in the picture, brother, this is what happened: I couldn't believe my eyes, there, holding forth among my guests, I suddenly saw that buffoon of a Chevalier. A lightning interrogation of the staff by Josefa revealed that the Chevalier had slipped into the house during the afternoon, disguised as a baker, supposedly delivering bread; then, with the help of a cook he had bribed and whom, of course, I'm going to fire, he hid in one of the larders, where he changed (and regaled himself), so that when the evening came he was already here. He assumed that once he was in I couldn't very well throw him out. He was wrong. I told Don Felix, who dealt with the matter very elegantly and without bloodshed, as you might say. He chose a moment when the Chevalier was nearby and then told the whole story, spicing it with a few nice details of his own. The assembled company creased up with laughter. A nervous tic appeared on the Chevalier's face, but I was the only one to notice that, since all other eyes were fixed on Don Felix. At the end, Don Felix raised his finger in the air and said, 'And the hero of my story is amongst us – here!' At which he pointed at the Chevalier.

How low will someone stoop, just to stay where things are happening and where there is food to eat! At first the Chevalier managed to control his tic and pretended that he would just grin and bear it. He made a few tired jokes and said, 'Oh no, oh dear, haha, half a loaf is better than no bread, haha, it'll all turn out for the best, I'm sure.'

But Don Felix assumed a very serious expression and said, 'Sir, you don't appear to realise when something is over. In your place I would leave.'

At that the Chevalier turned bright red and deathly pale by turns, he couldn't speak properly any more, and it was more of a whistle when he said, 'You will take back that lie . . .', and made as if to draw his sword.

Don Felix just laughed and said that he had once had a duel with a pug, but the dog did have an impeccable pedigree.

At that the Chevalier stormed out, snorting with indignation. Before he could go, however, I had a servant hand him his bundle. 'Don't forget your baker's outfit, Chevalier,' I said. 'You might need it another time.'

'He's not particularly well-disposed towards your Grace', said Don Picaza. 'I don't know if it was right to humiliate the man like that.'

'But he's a swindler . . .'

It's the truth. The fellow should be glad I didn't have him horse-whipped. In the first place he went snooping round my house, and in the second, I really have no sympathy with people who sneak in where they haven't been invited.

After that, Don Picaza left. I think I have already said that I have the feeling he is well-disposed towards me. And yet I do not know what to make of his visit. Who knows what kind of people there are in this Cancillería. Don Picaza's visit has certainly not reassured me. Whether it had anything to do with the fact that my fat cousin, Don Fernando, left the day before yesterday, I simply cannot tell.

At least I have got rid of my cousin for the moment. I spent a long time wondering what to do about him, and in the end I decided to give him 2,000 *reales*, telling him to regard them either as an advance on his inheritance, should the Duke be dead, or, should the Duke turn out to be still alive, as an interest-free loan over ten years. I have seldom seem anyone look so relieved as Don Fernando after that conversation. To give him his due, I must say that it was painfully obvious that it was not so much the money that pleased him as the prospect of being able to return home to his dragon of a wife bearing a visible token of success.

The whole company then left, looking rather different from when they arrived. His son, the pale, spotty Don Carlos Luis, was still picking his nose, it is true (he's a master of the art, he can stick both index fingers up his two nostrils at the same time), but the servants and horses had been fattened up, the coach-springs repaired (my wainwright saw to that), and the holes in their sleeves mended. Don Fernando was 2,000 *reales* the fatter, and his face was wreathed in smiles. They did leave one thing behind, however. One of his servants, his name is Lumbago, made a chambermaid of mine called Rosita pregnant, but he promised me he would come back in the spring, enter my service and marry Rosita. May the plague take him I said, if he didn't keep his promise.

I fear I won't be here any longer to see whether Lumbago keeps his promise.

I don't think anyone notices any more that I'm not Spanish. Even if I do still have an accent, it's obviously not one that stands out. You learn a language quickly when you are forced to use it all the time, even to think in it. I can understand everything, and I have the feeling that even unusual words just come to me. Of course, I imitate the manner of speaking of the person I talk to most, Josefa that is. I have Josefa's vocabulary. If it should ever come about that I travelled to Spain in your time, the people would probably just laugh at me, as if someone came to you speaking the German of Lessing's age. But I don't think, should I return, that I will ever come back here.

14th December Feast of
San Juan de la Cruz
Also the 3rd Sunday in Advent.

Don Picaza, the judge, has been here again, yesterday. In honour of San Juan de la Cruz, who was Prior here in Granada for a time, they burnt a young girl at the stake. When it is a *young* witch that is burnt, so Don Picaza tells me, the attendance at such an auto-da-fé is considerably increased.

That all sounds very dry and theoretical when you write it down like that. But it is difficult to describe how you feel when it is really going to happen. Naturally I didn't see the actual burning itself, but I did watch them bring the girl into the square. Of all places, they chose the square outside my house. It was at this point that Don Picaza arrived – thank God, I almost feel like saying. I'm still in quite a state. It is considered a a good work to watch an auto-da-fé, and secures you a few hundred years remission of purgatory. The Chaplain said I should consider myself fortunate it was happening outside our house as it also brings blessings on the house.

When they brought the girl, a pretty young girl, I felt as if the air were as transparent and fragile as glass. You just cannot imagine what it is like to know that this living being will be burnt to death. (Stephanie wrote, 'Is to be burnt', then crossed it out and wrote the stronger 'will be burnt' above it.) There is nothing as painful as fire. Don Picaza said it was possible she might still recant her heresy, in which case she will be strangled before she is burnt. If not, then –

Then what?

– then first of all she will be scorched with straw, what they call 'making a beard'. When they do that, the first thing to go up in flames is the *sanbenito*, the penitential robe which is all a female heretic has on, apart from the pointed hat, and that appeals to the male section of the audience in particular.

Now I knew why the Chaplain had been going around so excited all morning.

'How many people are burnt at the stake then, for God's sake?'

I asked.

'Not for God's sake', said Don Picaza, 'but to His Glory. Not many, your Grace, not many. Ten a year at most.'

'In Granada?'

'No, in the whole of Spain. Even the oldest people cannot remember the last big, really big, auto-da-fé. It was almost a hundred years ago, in 1680, when King Charles, of the Habsburg line, was still on the throne. My father, who was also a judge, attended it as a student. He went specially from Salamanca to Madrid, and made the whole journey on foot.'

'How horrible.'

'Not to see the heretics burn, but to further his career. The family he came from was of no consequence, and he had no connections. It was a great help to him throughout his life that he could say he had attended the great auto-da-fé of 1680. Had he not been such an important, well-respected judge, I doubt whether I would have been appointed to the post I have the honour to hold at the moment.

'In spite of that, you are not watching today?'

'I have to talk to you, your Grace.'

I could tell it was an excuse. Obviously he was disgusted by the public spectacle; just as obviously he couldn't admit it.

It was the afternoon. We were standing at the windows at the front. I had told Josefa I was only going to watch until they brought the poor thing into the square, and that not out of curiosity, but only so that at least one person would shed a Christian tear for her.

The crowd howled and jeered. They had built the bonfire in the morning. That in itself is a public festival too. Not just anyone can lay a faggot on it. It is an honour and a privilege.

Then they dragged in the supposed witch on a cart. She was wearing a tall, pointed cap and the *sanbenito*, a sackcloth robe reaching to the ground. The Bishop arrived beneath his baldaquin, followed by the clergy, incense, banners and singing. I can't help it, I just find it heathen. I hope that when the day comes the Devil will take all of those shouting and jeering down there, including the Bishop, all except the poor girl. But my Josefa too – she's not jeering, but wild horses couldn't drag her away from the window.

Then I left. I went as far away as I could, to a room at the back of the house. I went the moment the cart with the girl appeared round the corner of the square. I just gave it *one* glance. Fortunately that was the point at which Don Picaza arrived.

For all that he told me about it, he didn't know *why* the girl was being burnt at the stake. That, he said, was a matter for the ecclesiastical court. It was nothing to do with him.

Don Felix had asked me to let him watch from my window. I was aghast at the idea, but he didn't want to watch. That morning he had already got out of laying his own faggot on the bonfire. Another hidalgo had done it in his stead. It would have been noticed if he had not watched the fire, and he might even have been suspected of being a covert Protestant. As a Knight of Malta, he had received an invitation to sit in the Archbishop's stand, but he declined on the grounds that he had already received an invitation from me. I gave him a room to himself, with two windows looking out onto the square. No one will notice that he's not watching.

I am still in a state. I will try to write down my conversation with Don Picaza. I'm afraid I rather bungled it. Don Picaza was as polite as he was the first time, but it was perfectly clear that it was an interrogation rather than a conversation.

'Your Grace may rest assured that we, the members of the Cancillería, that is, see it as our foremost duty to help your Grace.'

'But why should I need the help of the members of the Cancillería?'

'His Grace, the Duke . . .' Don Picaza hummed and hawed at every word, 'had certain . . . habits.'

'You mean he was a womaniser?'

'Your Grace was unhappy with that?'

'What woman would be happy with it?'

'But perhaps, er, the first flames of passion were no longer burning in your Grace's heart?'

'I cannot remember ever having felt even the tiniest spark of passion for the Duke. I was married to him without having seen him beforehand.'

'And you talked this matter over with the Duke?'

'What? That I had not seen him before the marriage?'

'No, that there were certain aspects of the marriage between your Grace and the Duke about which, er, dispositions had to be made.'

'How do you know that?'

'That, your Grace, is beside the point. You confessed that you too felt a certain, er, had a certain, er, interest in a certain gentleman, and, to cut a long story short, you offered to tolerate his, er, how shall I put it . . .'

'Amours.'

'. . . his amours, if he for his part were prepared to, er, to overlook your partiality for the aforesaid gentleman. And you offered, even pleaded with him to sleep in separate rooms from that point onwards . . .'

'That's not true.'

'You insist it's not true?'

'I do.'

'But the Duke refused your offer, he even threatened to – please believe me, your Grace, when I say that I find it very difficult even to mention such matters to a person of high rank such as yourself.'

'There's no need to feel embarrassed. None of it's true.'

'Unfortunately we have proof.'

'Such as?'

As you can imagine, I was finding it difficult to conceal my horror. Of course everything was true, but how could the Cancillería know about a conversation between just the two of us? Especially now that one of us was dead? Don Felix was here, what I would really have liked to do would have been to call him. There I was, defenceless, and he was nearby, in the next room almost, not knowing the danger I was in. But to call him would have been the worst thing of all to do.

'Well', said Don Picaza, 'I do not have the authority to tell you that; however, we had it from an, er, aide of the

Cancillería. (He used the word *un secuaz*: a follower, a hanger-on, a spy.)

'And how does he know?'

'His Grace, the Duke told him.'

'And who is your' – I deliberately avoided *el vuestro secuaz*, saying instead *el vuestro afilar* – 'informer?'

'Don Giovanni Teodoro Gambini, Chevalier de Florimonte.'

'The swindler.'

'We have no proof that he is a swindler.'

'But I have', I lied. 'I have proof. He's a swindler. He's a fraud. He's no Florimonte and no Chevalier. A Gambini perhaps, a crook certainly. I have made enquiries.' That wasn't true, I made it up on the spur of the moment. 'He's an escaped jailbird. In Rome he was condemned to a long period of imprisonment . . .'

'Condemned?'

'. . . for fraud, for theft and' – I wanted to cap the list with something devastating – 'conspiracy against the rule of the Church in Italy.'

'But then . . . no, that can't be right, or he would have been condemned to death.'

'They didn't have a watertight case for the conspiracy charge, and anyway they reduced his sentence because he gave his accomplices away. He's got massive debts into the bargain. And he's not Italian, he's from Corsica, so he's French.'

'Since when have the Corsicans been French?'

'Corsica belongs to France, doesn't it?'

'Corsica has never belonged to France; whatever made your Grace think *that*?'

It was at that point that it occurred to me that I had perhaps said something wrong. You have to be so terribly careful when you know more of the future than other people. Doesn't Corsica belong to France yet?★

---

★ Corsica did not come under French rule until the treaty of the 15th May, 1768.

'Perhaps you're right', I said, 'I never was very good at geography.'

'The Chevalier found bloodstained bed-linen under a cupboard in a pavilion in the garden of your summer palace.'

'And it is the Duke's bed-linen?'

'A member of your household recognised it.'

'A member of my household? Anna?'

'Is your Grace calling your Dueña a swindler?'

'Did she recognise the Duke's blood?'

'Who would hide bloodstained bedclothes, if not a murderer?'

'And the Chevalier found them? And *how* did he come to find them? Perhaps he knew only too well, where they were hidden?'

'Are you saying it was the Chevalier himself who . . .'

'No', I said. I paused for effect and then went on, speaking slowly, 'No one murdered the Duke because the Duke is alive.'

I know it was an audacious stroke, but perhaps it was the right thing, the only thing left to try. Anyway, I gave myself no time to think about it, I said it the moment the idea came to me.

'The Duke is alive?'

'Yes. He's gone to America. The Viceroy of Nueva España is his cousin.' That much was true.

'And why has your Grace only told us that now?'

'Because I have only just learnt it myself.'

'And how did you learn this?'

'Because my husband sent me a letter from Vera Cruz.'

'Can I see the letter?'

'No.'

'Forgive me for asking, but why not?'

'The letter deals with . . . intimate matters that are of no concern to anyone apart from my husband and myself.'

'I can understand that, your Grace, but may I see the *outside* of the letter?'

'No. I am not prepared to show even the slightest glimpse

of the letter to a Cancillería which is clearly more prepared to believe a Corsican swindler than a Spanish Duchess.'

I know it was a weak argument, but I delivered it with an *hauteur* which surprised even myself and to which Don Picaza had little to offer in reply.

'Your Grace, er, if your Grace could perhaps see your way, er, not now, of course, but perhaps your Grace will reconsider – just the outside, a quick comparison of the handwriting, and then . . . We would be extremely relieved.'

'I will think the matter over, Don Picaza.'

'And, er, may I ask why his Grace has gone to Nueva España?'

'You may guess.'

'A mistress?'

'A mistress? Don't make me laugh! Four mistresses!'

The whole time I had noticed the smell of burning, but only with my nose, it had not penetrated my consciousness. It had found its way even into these rooms at the rear of the house. I lost my nerve, I admit it. Is it surprising?

'The girl's burning!' I screamed.

'What you can smell is the bonfire', said Don Picaza.

'No', I cried, 'it's the flesh I can smell!'

'You're mistaken . . .', said Don Picaza, but I left him where he was and dashed out.

When you realise that a living being is actually being burnt outside, reality gives way beneath you like mouldy floorboards. It wasn't the smell – I swear I could smell burning human flesh – that made my stomach heave. I felt as if the world were standing still, as if the air were made of glass. I had to get outside. I think I must have screamed terribly, 'Harness the horses! Don Felix!' I no longer cared who knew. The grooms were very unwilling to leave the windows, and especially the coachman and the two footmen who would have to sit on the box. The coachman was bewailing the remission of purgatory he would lose. He had to drive me out to our summer palace. I felt better as soon as I was out of the city.

Today, Sunday, I returned to the town house.

The smell had gone.

The priests know what they're doing when they make Hell a blazing inferno.

23rd December

I'll soon be returning to you. I've already written that I'm afraid of the way back. I'm also afraid that I won't be able to cope with your world any more.

Why did it have to happen to *me*? Did it happen because otherwise I wouldn't have met Don Felix? Have I always known him, without being aware of it? Or am I really the Duchess? I mean, is the Duchess real, and your sister, that Stephanie back there, only a shadow?

I can't stay here much longer. I know very well that the Cancillería will continue its investigations. Who knows how many other spies they have? The Chevalier de Florimonte has not reappeared in society, but Josefa heard that he's still here.

By the way, there was one not unimportant part of my conversation with Don Picaza that I forgot to write down. (Just now, for the first time since I've been writing things down, I had a look at the last section before starting again at the top of this page.) It didn't make any difference to the situation.

He confronted me with the fact that one Berundo, a notary, had been to the Cancillería. He had made a statement to the effect that a young female had asked him, on behalf of an unnamed person, what legal procedures would be set in motion if a Duchess were to murder her husband.

'There are several Duchesses in Granada', I replied.

'But only one whose husband has disappeared', said Don Picaza.

'How does your notary know it was a Duchess from Granada? If I wanted to make that kind of enquiry, I would have sent to Seville at least, if not farther.'

But I know very well that I can't stay much longer. I would like to stay just long enough to see Don Felix when he comes back from Madrid. He went there on the 15th. His

Order is holding some kind of convention during the Ember Days. Don Felix will be back before the New Year.

I'm wondering whether I shouldn't forge a letter, one that I can produce for Don Picaza as a letter from the Duke in America. It wouldn't be difficult. There are no such things as stamps or franking machines here. I would just have to try and copy the Duke's handwriting on the outside of a letter. In his desk I found papers, some of which Josefa recognised as being in the Duke's hand. Of course, I could always say that the address had been written by a secretary of the Duke's, not by the Duke himself. But in that case they would naturally want to see the inside of the letter. That could have been written by a secretary too, but it would make the excuse of all those intimate details seem rather implausible. To be on the safe side, Josefa has made surreptitious enquiries: there are two ships which docked in Cadíz during the time in question and which could have brought the letter, the *San Fernando* and the *Santa Clara*. Both ships have set out to sea once more, so an immediate check would be impossible.

Tomorrow is Christmas Day. Christmas Eve has no significance here. Over Christmas they hold large balls and *soirées*. I assume that during that period the Cancillería will not exactly be pursuing its investigations with restless energy.

Don Felix is not coming back to Granada at all. He has said his farewells to everyone already. He has received orders to return to Malta in early January. As the sea route is too dangerous in the winter, he has agreed – it was I who asked him – to travel overland as far as Naples and take a ship from there. I will never see him again; that is once he has left – he's coming back here on a clandestine visit. To the summer palace, not to Granada, that would be too dangerous.

I'm going to go out there to wait for him. I'll leave on St. Stephen's day. They'll all shake their heads, but I don't care, it makes no difference now.

I'll just take Josefa with me, one cook and two servants whom Josefa thinks are reliable. I don't know what would have happened to me here without Josefa.

### Saturday 27th

Something terrible has happened. Josefa has disappeared. And Don Felix still hasn't arrived. It was the cook who told me. Two men turned up and took her away. I asked why I wasn't told. The cook said hadn't I ordered some things we needed to be brought from Granada? I said, of course I had, but not that Josefa was to go herself. The cook said they thought it had been decided Josefa should go herself. Had she been dragged away by force, I asked. No, not really, the cook said, otherwise he would have thought there was something odd about it. He only thought it odd when I called for Josefa. Who the two men were? He didn't know them.

There's no doubt about it, Josefa's been taken away. And I'm afraid I know who gave the order.

I can't leave before Don Felix arrives. It will be the last time, anyway. Is that asking too much?

It's now five o'clock in the afternoon. I just don't know what to do. Should I return to Granada? Perhaps nothing's happened – yet.

But I can't go back to Granada, it's too late to drive back out here and Don Felix might arrive while I'm away.

If Josefa isn't back by tomorrow morning, I'll go. The servants can say what they like about it, I'll give instructions that no one is to be allowed into the palace, apart from Don Felix.

### Sunday, 28th December

I've been to Granada. It's worse than I feared. Josefa has been arrested.

When I got to the town house and they told me Josefa wasn't there, I drove like a fury to the Cancillería. I screamed and raged till those musty old rooms echoed to the sound of it. They were all dashing to and fro so that the air was filled with the powder from their wigs. Then Don Picaza came and led me into another room.

He was as polite as ever and said that he was still disposed in my favour, but had lost influence in the case. The opinion of the majority of the members of the Cancillería had turned against me. He begged me to produce the Duke's letter. I said I was prepared to do so if Josefa was freed immediately. (I have no idea what I would have done if they had accepted my offer. Something would have occurred to me, I'm sure.) Impossible, said Don Picaza.

Could I see Josefa?

No.

What right had they to hold Josefa?

To assist them in their inquiries.

Inquiries directed against myself?

Yes.

What were they doing to Josefa?

He couldn't reveal that.

He begged me to leave.

I was close to having another fit of rage, but Don Picaza very quietly advised me to remain calm, anything else would only harm Josefa. For the moment nothing would happen to her. In all probability she would soon be released.

Don Felix still hasn't come.

1st January; last letter.

It will be around ten o'clock in the evening. Don Felix is dead.

I have the ring on my finger, but I'm not going to go to bed before midnight. I'm being guarded, so it will not be easy to bury this notebook in the spot I've chosen. The judge – not Don Picaza, another one – has allowed me to spend one last night here in the room with the floral mosaic and in my bedroom. There are guards at the doors. However, they haven't noticed that the bedroom has a door out onto the terrace, the door I dreamt of that very first night.

From the judge's point of view, that's not a particularly serious dereliction of duty, since the whole palace is surrounded, all the gates of the estate. But I only want to go into the garden. I've already dug the hole, as deep as I could. No one must see me burying the notebook – I'll put it in the casket I keep my jewelry in, it's lined with metal on the inside – or of course they would immediately dig it up again. I think I should manage.

Don Felix came back on New Year's Eve. Whether the Chevalier de Florimonte knew that, or whether he was just snooping around on the off chance, I don't know. How he got into the house I can well imagine: the Chaplain was his accomplice. Without my knowledge and certainly without my order, he obviously came out here from Granada yesterday and was very careful to remain hidden all day.

Don Felix arrived shortly after midnight. As we had arranged, he knocked on the terrace door. (To climb over the park wall is easy for a man like him.)

Whether it was out of tact, or even a kind of consideration, I don't know, but the Chevalier did not make his entrance until Don Felix and I were at breakfast, here in the room with the floral mosaic.

Forgive me if I describe all this in plain, simple words, without any expression of the mourning I feel. I have no time left. I'm even writing it at the table at which Don Felix was sitting less than twelve hours ago, though I have moved it away from the place where they mopped up his blood.

I don't think there was any tact or consideration behind the timing of the Chevalier's arrival. I'm sure he would much rather have surprised Don Felix in quite a different situation. Most probably he was only called out by the Chaplain during the night. The murderer – the Chevalier, I'm past trying to think up an insulting way to describe him – rushed in with his sword drawn. The Chaplain stood outside with two loaded pistols and just stuck his head round the door.

'Since you only fight duels with pug dogs, you will not be interested in defending yourself against me', were the words of the murderer.

Then he ran his sword through Don Felix' throat. After Don Felix had collapsed to the floor, the Chaplain came in and fired one of his pistols at him, without, I think, hitting him.

I think I picked up the murderer's sword. I didn't have to draw it out of the wound; after Don Felix had fallen down, it was lying next to his body. I think I picked up the sword and threw myself at the Chevalier. At that, I think the Chaplain fired his second pistol at me, but I'm not sure. I can't properly remember everything which happened at that moment. If the Chaplain did shoot at me, then he didn't hit me. The two of them disappeared. I know that then the cook and one of the servants carried me back through the room with the floral mosaic and laid me on the bed in my bedroom. I came to again while they were carrying me, and I kept saying, 'It's all right, I can walk', but they still carried me.

Don Felix was still lying there. The whole of the floor was covered in blood. It's ridiculous, but the thing I registered above all was that the breakfast was still there on the table. I remember thinking that the chocolate in the cup that Don Felix had drunk out of was still hot.

In the afternoon the judge came, not Don Picaza, but another one. He told me his name but I've forgotten it. This judge is no less polite than Don Picaza, but he is not well-disposed towards me, which is hardly surprising since Josefa confessed everything under torture. I never thought of torture, that they might use torture, that torture still exists.

Josefa had not been seriously hurt, the judge told me, no permanent damage had been caused. Poor Josefa. I can't even leave her a legacy. Perhaps I'll give the cook — I hope he's honest — the three hundred and twenty-one gold coins I'll take out of the casket when I put this notebook in, and ask him to give them to Josefa. I know they cannot compensate her for the suffering I, in my selfishness, have caused her, but I know she is of a practical enough turn of mind to find some comfort in them. I really did not think of the possibility of them using torture. I could have done something about it if I had not insisted on waiting to see Don Felix again and had confessed to the murder as soon as they had arrested Josefa. I admit I was selfish enough to leave Josefa in prison for a few days, but I swear that it never occurred to me that they might use torture.

I must finish off my story.

I told the judge that everything Josefa had said was true. I said that I would go with him to Granada tomorrow of my own free will and make a confession to the Cancillería, that I would put myself in the hands of the Cancillería. As a favour, I asked to be allowed to spend this last night here in the palace.

The judge agreed.

Now I'm going to set off on my journey. The tube I have to pass through is so narrow. If at least the narrowest part were short, but it's dreadfully long. There's so much weight pressing down on it.

What will it be like when we meet again? What will I be like when we meet again?